THE EMPTY COFFINS

Two gruesome murders were discovered in the village of Little Payling. The bodies of a farmer and a local builder had been drained of blood. Their necks bore deep wounds, which centred on their jugular veins. When Scotland Yard arrived they made little progress — until Peter Malden became suspicious about his wife Elsie's first husband George Timperley, who had committed suicide. Then Elsie herself died and was buried — but her coffin, like George Timperley's, was found to be empty!

JOHN RUSSELL FEARN

THE
EMPTY COFFINS

Complete and Unabridged

LINFORD
Leicester

First published in Great Britain

First Linford Edition
published 2009

British Library CIP Data

Fearn, John Russell, *1908 – 1960.*
The empty coffins- -(Linford mystery library)
1. Detective and mystery stories.
2. Large type books.
I. Title II. Series
823.9'12–dc22

ISBN 978–1–84782–788–3

Published by
F. A. Thorpe (Publishing)
Anstey, Leicestershire

Set by Words & Graphics Ltd.
Anstey, Leicestershire
Printed and bound in Great Britain by
T. J. International Ltd., Padstow, Cornwall

This book is printed on acid-free paper

1

Eight Months To Live

In a small village there are invariably small minds, eager to seize on the slightest hint of scandal — and Little Payling, tucked away on the south coast, was no exception when it came to the case of Peter Malden and Elsie Timperley.

Elsie, a young widow of a month's standing, had been seen in the company of young Peter Malden for more times than seemed 'decent' considering Elsie's first husband was barely cold in the grave.

Tongues wagged, eyes watched from cottage windows, the local clergyman preached on the evils of carnal desire: in fact all Little Payling was concerned with a business which, strictly, was not its own.

'I hate Little Payling! I hate all the people in it! If I had the power to destroy them, I would!'

In this manner Elsie Timperley released

her feelings a fortnight after the hint-and-whisper campaign had begun against her. She strode the big drawing room of her house as she spoke, her mother, Peter Malden, and Dr. Meadows watching her in silence.

'Take it easy, dear,' Peter murmured, with an uneasy smile. 'After all, the folks in this place have never seen any further than their front gardens and they naturally think things.'

'Why *should* they?' Elsie twirled on her heel and faced Peter directly as he sat in the deep armchair by the fire. '*Why*? What are we doing that's wrong? We love each other and we mean to marry. What's so uncommon about that? After all, we've been friendly for years, long before George died.'

Silence. Elsie moved to the divan and sat down slowly, her fingers working in nervous irritation. She was a blonde girl of almost ethereal beauty. Though actually twenty-five she looked little more than eighteen. She had never seemed, even to her mother, to age with the years. The grace and lissomness of the adolescent had never left her. Blue-eyed, pink-cheeked, with a ruby-red mouth untouched by lipstick, she had more the appearance of an expensive doll than a human being.

'Perhaps,' Peter said at last, musing, 'we're moving too fast. We don't intend to marry for another four or five months — with all due respect to George — so why should — '

'I hated George!' Elsie flared at him, her eyes glinting. 'He was a beast! He made my life a misery. You know that particularly, Dr. Meadows.'

Dr. Meadows, slight, fiftyish, grey-haired, looked up with a start from contemplating the crackling fire. Outside the night was wild. The windows rattled under the buffeting of a rising winter gale.

'Yes, I know it, my dear,' he admitted, shrugging. 'He drank too heavily: he ill-treated you to the point of causing bruises and cuts which I had to patch up — Yet you never divorced him on the grounds of cruelty.'

Elsie glanced about her. 'I had only one reason for not doing. So that I could inherit all this. George had close on half a million pounds, most of which he told me would come to me when he died. I thought it better to put up with his abuses. Had I divorced him he would have hired the best lawyers to ensure I got as little as possible.'

Mrs. Burrows, Elsie's mother, gave a sigh. She was a stout, immovable woman, seated at the moment in the shadows just beyond the fireplace. Her eyes had been ranging from her neurotic, agitated daughter to Peter Malden. Peter, dark-haired, lean about the jaw, only just escaping being good-looking, had been listening mostly in silence, his gaze on the rug.

'George left you this fine house and a fortune,' Mrs. Burrows said at length. 'Whatever he may have been in life, Elsie, I think you ought to pay him a little more respect in death. The dead are all equal, remember.'

'What do you expect me to do?' Elsie asked. 'Go to his grave and weep upon it?'

'No. I just think you ought to wait a

4

year before marrying Peter, that's all. It would be more . . . delicate.'

Elsie was silent for a moment. A change had come over her expression. The anger died out of it and a wistful smile came instead.

'A year?' she repeated. 'I couldn't wait that long.'

'Why not?' her mother demanded. 'I'm sure Peter would, if he really loves you.'

'*If*!' Peter laughed. 'That's an understatement. Elsie knows I've loved her ever since the days we roamed the riverbanks together as kids. It just so happened that instead of things becoming a village romance — Elsie Burrows, as she was then, marrying Peter Malden, the local motor dealer and garage owner, she was swept off her feet by George Timperley instead. He blew in to build his housing estate, built this house in the meantime, and . . . married Elsie. But he's dead. It's all over. Elsie's right back where she started — except for the money she's had left her. Since Elsie knows I loved her long before the money came into things it shows I'm not just a fortune hunter.'

'We know you better than that, son,' Dr. Meadows said, smiling. 'I imagine you're not doing so badly yourself with that motor and garage business you've built up.'

'Yes, I can get by,' Peter admitted: and then he waited for Elsie to say something. Instead of doing so she remained looking into the fire, her wistful smile faded into a down-dragging of her mouth at the corners.

A sudden hurricane blast of wind against the windows made Dr. Meadows glance about him. He got to his feet deliberately.

'Time I was on my way.' he said. 'I've Mrs. Naysmith to see before I get home and I don't want to be out late on a night like this.'

'Good of you to come, doctor,' Elsie's mother said, also rising. 'You are quite convinced I have nothing worse than indigestion?'

'Quite!' Meadows' hazel eyes twinkled. 'You get that prescription made up and you'll be all right in no time — Now I really must be going. I had no intention of ever staying so long, but I could hardly refuse your hospitality and the wine . . . Well, good night, everybody.'

'I'll see you to the door,' Mrs. Burrows said, and followed him from the room.

The moment they were alone Peter got up and settled on the divan at Elsie's side.

'What's the matter?' he asked seriously. 'First you had such a lot to say — and now nothing. What's *wrong*?'

'Nothing.' Elsie replied, with a shrug.

'Then why don't you cheer up? After all, we arc going to be married — '

'But it's got to be before a year's up, Peter. It *must* be!' Elsie gripped his arm tightly. 'As soon as we possibly can.'

'That suits me fine. I've been advocating it all along. But I thought you were against it because of the villagers — '

'Hang the villagers! I can please myself, can't I?'

'That's what I'm hoping you'll do — ' Peter paused for a moment, obviously puzzled by something. He put his bands on Elsie's slim shoulders and forced her to look at him. 'Dearest, why this sudden wish for us to marry before a year is up?

What on earth difference does that make?'

She hesitated. 'I — I just don't want any delay, that's all. We're neither of us — getting any younger.'

Peter laughed incredulously. 'Great heavens, what a thing to say! Neither of us anywhere near thirty, yet you talk of us getting no younger — Honestly, dearest, there are times when I just don't understand you. Still, I suppose no man ever yet understood a woman thoroughly.'

With a click of the door latch Mrs. Burrows came back into the room. Coming to the fireplace she looked down on the two younger people pensively.

'In spite of the fact that I think you should both wait a reasonable time, in respect to the dead,' she said, 'I suppose you're still determined to get married as soon as possible?'

'That's right,' Elsie said quietly. 'After all, mother, it's for us to decide — not you.'

'I suppose so. I think you'd both do wisely to go away from here for a long holiday after your marriage. It will give the villagers less opportunity to talk.'

'I'm sick and tired of considering them!' Elsie cried, leaping to her feet again. 'I'll do as I like, and if I hear any scandal being breathed I'll have the law on them!'

'You could save it all by waiting perhaps a year,' her mother said. 'I cannot see what is so wrong in that. Twelve months isn't very long — '

'And lose my last chance of snatching a bit of happiness?' Elsie demanded tearfully.

Peter looked surprised. 'But, dearest, I'd wait. I've no interest in any other girl, and never have had.'

'It isn't that. It's — it's something else.' Elsie ran a hand distraughtly through her blonde hair. 'I can't explain. I'm probably horribly selfish, but I'm still human enough to want to snatch at life while it's still there. I've wasted so many years, when I was married to George, and now — '

She stopped, as though she found it impossible to find any more words to express her emotions. Peter got up and moved across to her. To his surprise he found her trembling when he put his arm about her.

'Elsie, what is it?' he asked quietly, and his hand gently pressing under her chin forced her to look at him. To his surprise there were tears drowning her blue eyes.

'What *is* it?' he insisted.

'I — I — ' she looked away and then apparently forced herself to speak. 'I'm going to die, Peter,' she whispered.

He did not speak, and neither did her mother. There was only the sound of the storm, the wind blowing through the gables of the house, rain pattering hard against the windows. A sudden billow of smoke came from the chimney and belched into the room.

'Die?' Peter repeated at last. 'Is that what you said? Die?'

Elsie nodded, but she did not speak.

'Stop being so utterly ridiculous!' her mother exclaimed, and it was hard for Peter to tell whether she was genuinely contemptuous or whether she hid fear under her sharpness.

'It isn't ridiculous!' Elsie retorted.

'How *could* it be? Certainly not for me! I said I was selfish — and I am. I wanted to marry you, Peter, so that before I die we can at least have a few months together . . . or at least I can. Now, I suppose, you'll think twice — and I wouldn't blame you.'

She turned away listlessly, but Peter caught her arm and drew her gently beck to him.

'I shall always want you, dearest, no matter how brief the time,' he said simply. 'But I refuse to credit this nonsense you're talking. You're only twenty-five, full of health and strength. Where on earth did you get the idea that you're going to die?'

'I was told so.'

'Who by? Dr. Meadows?'

'No. By Rawnee Singh, the mystic. He's naturally psychic and can see the future. He's featuring in the fun fair which is here for the Christmas holidays.'

Peter stared at her for a moment, then he burst into a laugh. It expressed, too, the overwhelming relief he felt.

'You actually mean you take notice of

some double-crosser in a sideshow? Why, you poor, foolish little fathead — '

'I'm not!' Elsie interrupted angrily. 'He's genuine. He told me all about myself — my past, and my future. He said he was very sorry but I have no future beyond the next eight months; and that can only mean — death. He was very kind and sympathetic and — '

'I should think he was,' Mrs. Burrows interrupted dryly. 'How much did he charge for his infamous opinion?'

'Ten pounds. I went over to the fair last night — and I quite enjoyed myself until I went in to see him. I wish to heaven I'd never gone. I wouldn't have done, only you had a breakdown job last night, Peter, and you couldn't join me.'

Peter gave a grim look. 'Elsie, the sooner you stop believing a lot of claptrap the better. You allow things to upset you too easily. The villagers' gossip, for instance, and now this idiot, who claims to know the future — I know what I'm going to do. I'm going down there to have a word with him this evening, and I'm not so sure I shan't bring an action against him for upsetting you like this.'

'But Peter, he's genuine,' Elsie insisted. 'How could he read my past like he did if he weren't?'

'I dunno. These sideshow merchants are up to all the tricks. Anyway. I'm going to see him — *now*. Want to come with me?'

Elsie shuddered. 'Not at any price. I just couldn't bear to look at the man again. He's so strange — and yet so gentle. So — other-worldly.'

'Maybe a good punch in the nose will even him up,' Peter snapped, then he relaxed a little and gave the girl a kiss. 'Now stop worrying, sweetheart. I'll be back later and let you know what happened. If it should be very late I'll give a ring instead. In any case I'll be here tomorrow evening as usual and we'll keep that theatre date in Branscombe.'

He said good night to Mrs. Burrows, and Elsie saw him as far as the door. Her face, with the pink cheeks and tearful eyes, made him smile encouragingly.

'Such rubbish,' he chided, patting her arm. 'When you're ninety you'll tell this

13

piffle to your great-grandchildren.'

With that he opened the door and a hurricane blast of wind and rain smote him. Wrapping his coat collar up round his ears he went down the steps to his waiting saloon and clambered into it. In a moment or two he was driving down the wide driveway of the house and gained the main road into the village a few seconds later.

The night was the foulest he had known for some time. The leaf-bare trees at the side of the road, clearly illumined by the car headlights, were bending double in the fury of the gale. Rain splashed in torrents down the windscreen. Back and forth clicked the wiper, leaving a clear view ahead through the segment it cut into the downpour.

Then Peter gave a start of surprise. Ahead of him, drawn to the side of the lane, was a car. Leaning into the engine, flashing a torch, was a man's figure. As he came nearer Peter recognized the car as Dr. Meadows', and the man was Meadows himself.

'What's wrong, Doc?' Peter pulled up

14

and lowered his driving window. 'Run into trouble?'

Soaked, rain dripping from his soft hat, Meadows came over the pool-swamped roadway.

'Engine trouble. Wet probably. Mind giving me a tow in?'

'I'll do better than that. Hop in before you get even wetter. I'll run you home then I'll have my garage boys come and pick your car up. How about Mrs. Naysmith? Still got to see her?'

Meadows climbed in beside Peter and slammed the door.

'She can wait. Nothing important, anyway, and I'm too wet to bother at the moment. Just drop me at home, son, if you don't mind.'

'Okay — providing you don't object to a little detour. You live just beyond the village on the other side: I'm calling at the Christmas fun fair on the way.'

Peter began driving forward again and Meadows shook his head irritably as rain trickled from his hat into his lap.

'The fun fair?' he repeated. 'What on earth for?'

'I've a man to see. He's been scaring Elsie to death.'

'Oh? Will the fair be open on a night like this?'

'Should be. Most of it's under canvas.'

Meadows took off his hat and examined it in the dashboard light.

'How do you mean, frightening Elsie? Assault or something? There's the law you can — '

'The law can't touch this, Doc. He's a mystic, or some such humbug. Rawnee Singh, by name. He told Elsie that she cannot live any longer than eight months from now — and she, poor kid, believed the swine! That was why she was so insistent tonight that we be married before a year is up. She's got some crazy idea of snatching at happiness before she dies. I never heard such damned, nonsensical piffle!'

Meadows sat back in the bucket seat and returned his hat to his head. He was silent, gazing through the raindrops at the headlamps' glare on the lane. Presently Peter gave him a glance.

'You think it's crazy, Doc, don't you?'

he asked, in some surprise.

'I suppose it is,' Meadows admitted, shrugging. 'You can't trust these sideshow mystics.'

'You don't sound unduly angry. Suppose Elsie were your daughter? Wouldn't you want to set about this lunatic and maybe rub his face in the mud?'

'It would be easier if I didn't know Singh's reputation,' Meadows replied, frowning. 'Rawnee Singh isn't just a sideshow charlatan, Peter: he's been giving psychic demonstrations to society for many years. I've seen accounts of his activities. As for him being at this local fair, it's because his name is the main attraction . . . Quite an extraordinary seer, from what I can gather.'

Peter drove through the village with its lighted windows and rain-lashed streets before he spoke again.

'But, Doc, in regard to Elsie, you surely don't think — '

'Good Lord, no! It's fantastic . . . There's the fair ahead of us, all lit up. Business as usual despite the rain, I gather. Want me to come with you?'

'Why not? As an older man, I'd value your opinion on this character.'

Meadows nodded and climbed out of the car, leaving it behind on the big cindery enclosure that was doing temporary duty as a carpark.

Then, driven along stumblingly by the wind, turning their faces from the blinding rain, they hurried towards the huge mass of gleaming canvas ahead of them. It was lighted by clusters of electric globes, their naked glare reflecting from wet surfaces.

Beyond the outer flap of the gigantic marquee they found relief from the wind and rain. It was warm and bright and smelled of sawdust and people. All the men and women of the village seemed to be present, walking up and down the narrow aisles between the sideshows. The din was overwhelming, the basic noise coming from amplified music connected with a roundabout.

'Over there,' Meadows said, nodding. 'There's his sign.'

Peter studied a garish board saying RAWNEE SINGH KNOWETH PAST

AND FUTURE; then he followed Dr. Meadows as he pushed his way through the crowd.

Gaining audience with the mystic was by no means an easy job. Business seemed to be brisk for him. It meant waiting with several other people in an outer tent, whilst an attendant with nut-juice on his face and hands and wearing Oriental costume kept coming in and out of a second tent and giving a deep obeisance.

Finally, however, Peter and Meadows found themselves in the presence of the seer — after they had paid their money to the pseudo-Oriental. The sanctum of Singh was blue with incense fumes and lighted only dimly by candles. Their indifferent flames cast upon strange carvings and fantastic shapes. Rawnee Singh himself sat cross-legged before a low table, his slender hands over a softly illumined globe. A turban with satiny sheen graced his head and his close-fitting suit had the appearance of cloth-of-gold.

'Good evening, gentlemen,' he greeted, his voice bass and musical. 'Please be seated and state your pleasure. Is it the past you wish to recover, or perchance do you prefer to gaze into the future?'

'I'm concerned only with the present — or rather last night,' Peter retorted, remaining standing with Meadows beside him. 'You've almost scared my fiancée to death with your damned tosh!'

Singh raised his head. His face was dark brown, his eyes oblique in shape and brightly gleaming. It was a satanic face, with its downwardly curved mouth and vulture's nose.

'Take care how you speak,' he whispered. 'The spirits show no mercy to the infidel.'

'You didn't show any to my fiancée,' Peter retorted. 'Maybe you remember her? Elsie Timperley by name. You told her she had only eight months to live — What the devil did you mean by it?'

Rawnee Singh meditated, his eyes on the glowing ball in his hands. Then he seemed to remember.

'Ah yes — the blonde young lady. She came last night — Yes, of course, I remember. But, Mr. Malden, I spoke truth.'

'How do you know my name?' Peter asked suspiciously.

'I am psychic. Do I need to say more?'

'Definitely you do! Why did you scare Mrs. Timperley?'

'It was unavoidable. She asked for the future, and I revealed it to her — just as I revealed her past. Naturally she cannot feel happy over the revelation that she has only eight months — maybe less — to live.'

'Damned lies!' Peter shouted, leaning across and gripping Singh by the front of his costume. 'For two pins I'd — '

He paused. Magically, from the shadows, two enormous Nubians had appeared, their mighty arms folded. They stood like black statues, as straight as the columns of hell, and probably just as diabolical if they chose. Peter relaxed and stood up straight again.

'I regret your recourse to violence, Mr. Malden,' Singh said, straightening his costume. 'I can only repeat: I gave Mrs. Timperley the facts.'

'But you couldn't have meant it!'

'The gods do not lie, Mr. Malden.'

Peter gave a desperate look about him. The smoky tent, the Oriental setting, the giant Nubians with folded arms, and this immovable mystic with his glowing globe. The whole business smelled either of rank faking or else profound sorcery. Peter could not tell which. Finally he asked a question.

'*How* will she die? Did you work that one out?'

Singh gave the slightest of shrugs. 'There was no purpose in doing so, my friend. All I could see ahead of her, after the passage of eight months, was a blank. That, interpreted, means death. How it will come about I do not know: I made no effort to probe. I can discover that if the lady cares to come again and — '

'Not on your life! You've frightened her enough already.'

'Mr. Singh,' Meadows said quietly, 'I have read of your reputation. I am not as impetuous as my young friend here. I would like to ask: is there not the possibility of you having made a mistake?'

'I perhaps, yes,' the mystic admitted. 'I am but the poor mortal tool for the forces that move around me. I am, shall I say, only an interpreter of past and future. I could have made a mistake, but the forces themselves would not. So you may take it for granted I spoke truth. I am very sorry, gentlemen. I feel it as deeply as you that a young woman, so lovely in every way, should be doomed to extinction. It is hard sometimes to understand the laws of destiny.'

'You *can't* feel it as deeply as we do,' Peter snapped. 'You're a total stranger. Mrs. Timperley doesn't mean a thing to you.'

'True, but I am still a human being. I try to be sympathetic towards the emotions of others . . . ' Singh turned and motioned his Nubian servants out of the tent, then looking back at Peter and Meadows he asked, 'Perhaps you two gentlemen would care to know how your own destiny will work out?'

'No thanks,' Peter answered curtly.

'As you will. I would remark that both of you are surrounded by a strange aura. It is otherworldly, spawned of the darkness . . . Surely you two gentlemen, loving Mrs. Timperley as you both do, wish to know your future?'

Peter gave a little start of surprise. 'As we *both* do?' he repeated. 'You're all mixed up, Singh. I'm the one who is in love with Mrs. Timperley. This is — '

'I know — Dr. Meadows,' the mystic interrupted, with a slow smile. 'You also love Mrs. Timperley, my friend. Your mind speaks the fact to me.'

'It's time we got out of here,' Meadows said abruptly, a shadow crossing his usually genial face. 'Come on, Peter. Thanks for the information, Mr. Singh.'

The mystic said nothing. Impassively he watched the two men leave the 'sanctum.' They passed through the outer tent and then into the din and blazing lights of the main marquee. Before they plunged out once more into the fury of the night Peter caught the doctor's arm.

'What did he mean, Doc?' he demanded. 'About both of us loving Elsie? That statement was as crazy as the rest of his bosh, wasn't it?'

'No,' Meadows said, and gave Peter a direct look. 'I am inclined to think that everything he said was accurate, including his remark about me.'

'But you can't mean that you love Elsie too?' Peter gave an incredulous laugh. 'Why, it's absurd! You're a middle-aged man, old enough to be her father, and — '

'I am twenty five years older than Elsie,' Meadows interrupted. 'That still doesn't stop me loving her, does it? I have always been in love with her. There was a time, when I was treating her for the injuries that swine George Timperley had inflicted when I felt I . . . ' Meadows stopped and gave a grave smile. Then he clapped Peter on the shoulder.

'Let's say no more,' he said. 'I love her, and I always shall, but as is only natural she has chosen you — so much nearer her own age. Elsie is the one reason I have never married. To me, the barrier of years between us is the biggest curse.'

'Marriages with twenty five years difference between the partners are not uncommon,' Peter said, thinking.

'I know — but the choice is Elsie's. I don't think she knows how I feel about her, and now you have her she never will.'

Peter was silent for a moment, then he frowned.

'Do you realize, Doc, that if Singh was right on that point, regarding you I mean, he might be on the other one? About Elsie — dying, that is.'

'His reputation is sufficient to make me believe it,' Meadows answered slowly. 'Which leads to an obvious conclusion. Elsie should submit to a medical test to discover if she has any kind of trouble that could end her life in the prescribed time. If she is perfectly normal, then the only other answer is an accident — which we cannot possibly foresee or prevent.'

'We might,' Peter said, clenching his fists.

'No, son, it couldn't be done. You can't alter destiny — ' Meadows put finger and thumb to his eyes for a moment and then sighed. 'We'd better be getting along,' he finished. 'We've had quite enough shocks for one night — and you have still to give instructions to have my car towed in.'

2

Vampire Attack

Peter, once he had driven Dr. Meadows home and then attended to the matter of his car, went back to the Timperley residence to inform Elsie of what had happened. She and her mother were both still in the drawing room and they listened in silence to all Peter had to say.

'It's all so crazy,' he finished, pacing up and down in his gleaming mackintosh. 'I don't want to believe it, and yet I have to. There's only one way to settle it, Elsie: let Dr. Meadows examine you.'

'And make certain of my fate?' Elsie glanced up in the firelight and shook her head. 'No, Peter. That I will never do. I intend to cling to the one thought that Singh is wrong and that I will go on living, through the years. You and I, as it should have been had not George butted in and upset things.'

She got to her feet and moved to where Peter was standing. Her hand rested lightly on his.

'Then we go ahead and marry — as planned?' he asked.

'As soon as possible. Most certainly I refuse to try and discover how I am to die. It is bad enough to be told it will come about so soon without knowing just how . . . Or perhaps,' Elsie finished, her hand lowering, 'you would prefer to back out now there is this cloud over us?'

Peter shook his head. 'All the more reason why I should stand by you. I'll make all the arrangements and we can be married within a month.'

Elsie's mother, seated by the fireplace, said nothing but her mouth tightened a little. Peter hesitated over telling Elsie of Dr. Meadows' own regard for her, then he thought better of it. Things were difficult enough for her without more being added.

'I'll be here tomorrow,' he said, turning away actively. 'By then I'll have made the first moves . . . Try not to worry, dearest. I'm sure it's all crazy.'

He kept up his reassurances all the way to the front door, where he kissed the girl good night — but once he was in his car again in the raging fury of the storm all the old fears came surging back into him. He could not shake free the feeling that doom, from somewhere, somehow, was reaching out to strike the girl down.

Half way back to the village, where his house was attached to the garage, he was jerked out of his moody preoccupation. It happened just as he was passing the cemetery on the village outskirts. The car headlights picked up the desperately running figure of a young girl, hatless, without overcoat or mackintosh, her simple frock plastered to her figure by the swamping rain. At the sound of the car and glare of its headlights she stopped and waved a hand frantically.

Peter drew to a halt with a shriek of brakes, the tires locked in the wet gravel. He opened the door quickly and looked at the girl's white, rain-dewed face. Her dark hair was flattened to her head and dripping with water.

'What in the world's wrong?' Peter

asked in amazement. 'Hop in . . . I can give you a lift.'

'T-thanks.' She scrambled into the seat beside him and slammed the door. Then she sat breathing hard and gulping whilst Peter looked at her curiously.

'I believe I know you,' he said finally. 'You live in the village here, don't you? Why, of course? You're Madge Paignton, from the grocery shop? I hardly knew you with your hair all wet.'

'Yes — I'm Madge Paignton,' the girl agreed breathlessly. 'I — I was attacked a little while back — In the cemetery there.'

'*Attacked*?' Peter's tone changed. 'By whom? Or don't you know?'

'I've not the least idea.' Madge Paignton began to get a grip on herself, but she was shivering in her wet clothes. 'I — I'd been to see a friend the other side of the cemetery in Kingsford Row. Y-you know where that is? I cut through the cemetery coming home because I was late — I'd got halfway then somebody — or something — attacked me. I had a terrible time. My coat was torn off; I lost my hat. I'm sure I'm covered with dozens of scratches and bruises, particularly on my neck . . . ' She fingered it tenderly. 'Then I tore free somehow and ran — and ran — After that you caught up with me.'

Peter tugged out a rug from the back of the car and wrapped it about her shoulders. Then he restarted the engine.

'Better get you home, young lady,' he decided. 'You can tell your story by a warm fire. I'll pick up Dr. Meadows and the police on the way.'

The girl gave him a grateful smile and he started the car forward again into the storm. Twenty minutes later the girl was in the kitchen of her simple home, her father, mother, and her younger sister looking on in wonder — and anger — as she told her story. Wrapped in a dressing gown and beside a warm fire, coffee in the cup in her hand, she gave the details, haltingly at first — then with greater fluency.

By the table Dr. Meadows listened, apparently trying to puzzle things out for himself. The 'police' were represented by the solid, none-too-bright personages of

Sergeant Blair and Constable Hawkins. Their powers did not run much beyond dealing with thefts from an orchard.

'What did this attacker look like, Madge?' Peter asked presently, when the girl had repeated the story she had told him.

'I don't know,' she answered, frowning. 'It had no sort of shape, somehow.'

'*Must* have had,' Sergeant Blair said heavily. 'It certainly wasn't a ghost, anyway. A ghost couldn't have scratched your neck like that.'

He motioned to the plasters Dr. Meadows had affixed to the girl's neck, low down under the hair-line. On her throat, too, there had been two gashes close to the jugular on each side, but neither of them serious.

'He was all in white,' Madge said at last. 'A hideous looking man with no expression on his face. And terribly strong! I was flung to the ground. It wasn't strength that enabled me to get away. I got in a lucky kick somehow and found myself free for a moment — So I got up and ran.'

'And that's all you can tell us?' Blair asked, puzzled.

'I'm afraid it is, Sergeant.'

Dr. Meadows stirred a little and locked up his bag. Then: 'Do any of you people here believe in vampires?'

There was a dead silence for a moment, one looking at the other. Sergeant Blair licked the end of his pencil and turned bovine eyes upon the doctor.

'Yes, it sounds ridiculous,' Meadows admitted, shrugging. 'But the fact does remain that these injuries of Madge's are similar to those which a vampire might inflict. It is plain that some creature or other had tried to pierce the main veins on her neck, particularly the jugular. Fortunately the attempt failed. An ordinary attacker would not do a thing like that. She would have been hit over the head, probably.'

'But this is preposterous!' Peter exclaimed. 'A vampire doesn't really exist! It belongs to folklore. It's as crazy as fairies at the bottom of the garden!'

'Is it?' Meadows gave a faint smile. 'I'm not sure of that, Peter. In many small villages in England, such as this one — places rich in folklore and legend — apparitions have been seen from time to time. Ghosts, creatures of tiny stature, which might even be gnomes, and vampires. Look through the history of any village, this one included, and you'll find all the details. For my own part — and I've studied the subject — I believe that vampires *do* exist. After all, why not? We have definite evidence that ghosts and presences appear amongst us. Why not vampires?'

Sergeant Blair scratched the back of his ear. 'Beggin' your pardon, doctor, but just what *is* a vampire, anyway? Is it one of those bat-things?'

'No.' Meadows shook his head. 'You're thinking of a vampire-bat — a different thing altogether. It's a bat belonging to Central and South America. A vampire proper is the ghost of a suicide, or some such excommunicated person, who seeks vengeance on the living by attacking them and sucking away their blood. The person attacked also becomes a vampire in turn and preys upon others as he himself was preyed upon.'

Sergeant Blair licked his lips and Constable Hawkins' Adam's-apple moved grotesquely up and down as he swallowed.

'Great heavens!' Madge Paignton shrieked, leaping up and holding her throat. 'You don't mean that *I* might — '

'Good heavens, no, child.' Meadows gave a serious smile and walked over to her, giving her shoulders a reassuring squeeze. 'You've nothing to worry about — though you might have had if you had been genuinely bitten . . . I may be wrong in my theory, of course — I sincerely hope I am — but I still think it's worth considering.'

'Best thing we can do,' Sergeant Blair decided, 'is go to the cemetery and see what we can discover. This amounts to a criminal attack on Miss Paignton and we've got to find out who did it — I don't suppose you'd care to come too, doctor? Knowing about — vampires, I mean?'

Meadows shrugged. 'I will if you wish. Have you got your car with you? Mine's — '

'You can use mine,' Peter said. 'It's outside. I think we'd better all go and have a look.'

He led the way to the door and the doctor and two police officials followed him. Perhaps ten minutes later Peter had drawn up outside the cemetery's locked gates. He clambered out into the rain, Meadows and then the two policemen emerging after him.

'No night for a job like this,' Blair growled, and he glanced up at the leaf-empty trees lashing in the screaming wind.

'The law has to act, even if it be in the midst of an earthquake,' Meadows said. He fumbled in his pocket and brought a small torch to view in the glow of the sidelights from Peter's car. 'Here, Sergeant: this may be useful.'

'Thanks.' Blair contemplated the gates, gleaming with rain. 'How d'you suppose we get into this damned place? Climb the railings?'

'Only way, I imagine.' Peter responded. 'I suppose Madge Paignton must have done that since the gates are closed . . . I'll go first.'

He grabbed onto the ironwork, thrust his foot into one of the ornamentations, and then clambered upwards. The policemen followed him, and they in turn gave a hand to Dr. Meadows, for whom it was no easy task. Finally, however, the quartet was on the other side of the barrier and walking along the main shale pathway leading to the little church. To either side of them, glistening with rain as the torch-beam struck them, loomed gravestones, tablets, and pillars.

'There must be an easier way in and out of this place,' Blair said presently. 'That girl said she used this cemetery as a short cut. She'd hardly climb railings at both sides — and in her Sunday-go-to-meeting clothes too. We'd better look for the spot where she must have got through — the one nearest Kingsford Row.'

They found an opening ultimately, well beyond the church itself and at the other side of the graveyard to the spot at which they had entered. Here the railings were partly collapsed and apparently the slovenly local authority had been at no pains to put them back up again.

'Yes, this is where she must have entered,' Blair said, flashing the torch beam around him on gravel and gravestones. 'We'd better work our way across and see if we can locate the spot where she was attacked. Pity she wasn't more specific — but I suppose she was too scared to remember.'

The other men did not speak. They glanced about them as they walked, turning their faces as much as possible from the deluge sweeping across the dreary expanse of burial ground — then presently Dr. Meadows stopped and pointed.

'What's that?' he asked, and Blair swung round the torch beam. It settled on something black with rain lying at the edge of the shale pathway.

'Madge Paignton's overcoat,' Constable Hawkins said, picking it up. 'Here's her name stitched on the lining.'

Meadows, Peter, and Blair moved to the spot. At this point the grass verge joined the pathway. There were obvious signs of there having been a struggle — gouges in the shale, lumps of turf kicked up, and on a nearby grave some flowers had been overturned and the topsoil was indented with footprints.

'Apparently Miss Paignton spoke the truth,' Blair looked about him. 'All the signs of it. Footprints and — '

'Not only her footprints, either,' Meadows said, studying the grave's soil surface. 'Look at this! Shoe marks, and those of naked feet.'

'*Naked*?' The Sergeant gave a start and bent to a closer examination. Constable Hawkins and Peter looked also — then all four men glanced at each other in wonder. There was no doubt of the fact that naked feet had pranced about on the topsoil.

'What do you make of it, doctor?' Peter asked, puzzled.

'I'm afraid it verifies my theory,' Meadows answered, frowning. 'Obviously a vampire would not wear shoes. The creature is supposed to arise from the grave, through the coffin and the surrounding soil, to desecrate the living. The creature concerned would be barefooted and in a shroud.'

The howl of the wind whipped away some further words he added. Sergeant Blair licked his lips and gave a furtive glance.

'Do you suppose we could — *find* this vampire?' he asked. 'Granting it exists?'

'From the look of these footprints. Sergeant, there is little doubt as to its existence. As for finding it — ' Meadows gave a shrug. 'That, I am afraid, is impossible. A vampire has the power to vanish as completely as a ghost, returning maybe to the grave from which it came.'

'And which grave do you suppose that could be?' Constable Hawkins demanded.

Meadows looked about him on the lonely tombs, the wind howling dismally past them.

'I've no idea,' he said at last. 'How can I have?'

Blair cleared his throat. 'I don't like this blasted business a bit,' he admitted frankly. 'I'll tackle anything that belongs to this world — anything flesh and blood; but when it comes to crawly things that come out of a grave — I don't want any part of it!'

'If it's in your line of duty you'll have to put up with it,' Meadows told him. 'We're up against something supernatural — judging from the evidences — and it's your job to discover exactly what, or who, it was which attacked that girl. All the village will demand to know. It may not have been the only attack. If a vampire *is* loose in this cemetery nobody is safe, from the youngest to the eldest.'

'Then what do I do?' Blair demanded. 'I can't chase something that doesn't exist!'

'It *does* exist, Sergeant — only it has the power to return to its starting point. Namely, the coffin from which it came. However, maybe there is a way of getting at it . . . '

The other men waited, huddled against the buffeting wind and streaming rain.

'A vampire,' Meadows proceeded, 'is technically a spirit, an evil presence. In its waking moments when it becomes a vampire it is visible much the same as when alive as a human being, except that it will wear a shroud. But, upon returning to the grave whence it came, it becomes invisible to mortal eyes because it is in a state of suspended animation. For the time being, that is, it is not pervaded by the demoniac life it possesses when on the rampage. Which means that wherever in this cemetery there is a totally empty coffin — there lies the vampire.'

'Oh!' Blair said, and the whites of his eyes showed as he glanced at Hawkins.

'If it's not there,' said Hawkins, 'how do we kill it?'

'Obviously you can't, if it's invisible. The only thing to do is wait until it is on the rampage — and visible — Then attack it and drive a stake through its heart. There is no other way.'

'It — it doesn't seem to be anywhere about tonight,' Hawkins said, with a glance around the dismal spaces. 'So I suppose we'd better hold a nightly vigil here, starting tomorrow night, to see if we can locate this — thing.'

'You can try that, of course,' Meadows agreed. 'But please remember that vampires do not necessarily haunt the churchyard. They move far and wide over the countryside. They can strike — any-where.'

'But they have to *start* from the churchyard,' Peter pointed out. 'It seems the best place to me.'

'That is up to our two good friends here,' Meadows said. 'For my part I'm having nothing to do with the business. I've read enough to know what horror a vampire can inflict on a hapless human being. I don't intend to lay myself open to possible attack.'

'We'd better get out of here,' Blair decided. 'Maybe we'd better ask some-body from the Institute of Psychic Research to come down here and look the place over. Vampires are hardly in the line of police duty.'

'That's up to you,' Meadows said. 'I'd add, though, that psychic investigators are more concerned with phantoms and poltergeists than vampires.'

Nothing more was said as the journey through the cemetery continued. When presently the railings were reached a search was made to find an opening, through which Madge Paignton had presumably escaped. It was discovered finally: two railings being twisted apart far enough to permit the passage of a body.

'Well, that's that,' Peter said, when they were back in the roadway with his car twenty yards distant. 'Can I give you a lift home, doctor? You too, gentlemen?'

They all nodded their thanks in the glow of the torch, but said nothing. The sobering effect of the churchyard and Dr. Meadows' observations had made speech singularly difficult.

Peter led the way back to his car and dropped the two police officers in the village; then he carried on beyond it with Dr. Meadows seated beside him.

'All this talk about a vampire isn't just a — a leg-pull, is it, doc?' Peter asked, after a while.

Meadows gave him a glance. 'Good heavens, Peter, you know me better than that! I'm convinced it is all too true — and that's why I'm worried. With a vampire loose, just anything can happen until it is destroyed.'

'I find it hard to believe in anything so hideous.'

'That's because you have never encountered it before. To you it probably seems as remote from possibility as a sea-serpent.'

'More so. I'm afraid.'

'Such things do exist, son,' Meadows said deliberately. 'I know they do. You see — my cousin died because of an attack by a vampire.'

Peter nearly released the steering wheel in his amazement.

'He — did?'

'It wasn't in this country,' Meadows continued soberly. 'At that time I was practicing in a remote corner of Ireland, and if ever there was a place for manifestations it is Ireland. I was staying with my cousin at the time. He was attacked one night by something he could only describe as deathly white, which seemed to float through the air. On his neck were two scars. From the night of that attack he began to waste away, and finally died.

'At first we thought he had some kind of disease — we being myself and the villagers amongst whom I was living — then it occurred to somebody that he

45

was perhaps being attacked nightly by a vampire which was drawing the blood from his body. It was only then that he had consciousness enough to describe the nightly visit of the white apparition. He had thought it a dream: we knew it was fact. We killed the vampire finally by driving a stake through its heart when it came one night. My cousin died shortly afterward. Presumably he too became a vampire — I didn't wait to see. I left Ireland post haste and came to England here.'

Peter drew up the car outside the doctor's home.

'I think,' Meadows said, climbing out into the rain and drawing him bag after him, 'we're up against it, son. Quite a lot of unpleasant things may happen in this village of ours before we're much older.'

'Unless the vampire is caught.'

'Hope for the best . . . Good night, Peter, and thanks for the lift — both ways.'

Meadows slammed the car door and went up the front door to his house. Peter sat thinking for a moment, the windscreen wiper clicking back and forth steadily; then he reversed the car and drove back through the streaming rain to his home.

3

The Empty Coffin

The mysterious attack that had been made on Madge Paignton was not repeated on any other member of the village, either man or woman. For some nights, Sergeant Blair and Constable Hawkins kept a watch on the cemetery, but nothing happened. So, gradually, things began to drift back to their former state of torpor and there was no more talk of vampires or things that go bump in the night.

Peter said nothing to Elsie of his experience. The girl was under strain enough; but inevitably, during her visits to the village, she heard of the vampire and its supposed attack on Madge Paignton. Not that she paid much heed: she seemed to consider such fantasy as not worthy of notice.

Peter for his part went ahead with the

wedding arrangements, and a month after his experience with Madge Paignton he and Elsie were married. They honeymooned in London and returned to Little Payling a month afterwards. By this time the worst inclemency of winter had passed and February was passing into March.

Upon their return they both expected to hear gossip about themselves, but instead it centered upon a totally different subject — one they had both believed had expired. Vampires! Or at least, one vampire.

The facts, as far as they could glean them in the village, were that during their absence two more attacks had succeeded. A farmer — and a week later, a well known local builder — had both been foully murdered. Apparently their bodies had been discovered almost drained of blood. The farmer had been found in a ditch, and the builder in a pond. In both cases the men had deep wounds at either side of their necks, centring exactly on the jugular veins.

Scotland Yard had been busy, uprooting

everything right and left and questioning nearly everybody in the village; but they had arrived at no concrete conclusion.

'And now,' Dr. Meadows said, shrugging, 'the matter seems to have lapsed.'

He had come over for one of his routine examinations of Mrs. Burrows, who was still convinced her dyspeptic flutterings were connected with heart trouble.

'You mean,' Peter asked, amazed, 'that the Yard have let the whole thing drop?'

'Little else they can do,' Meadows closed up his bag as it stood on the drawing room table. 'Naturally, Blair and Hawkins found the business beyond them in no time, so the Yard had to be called in. I think the reason's pretty clear: they just don't believe in a vampire. They prefer to look for a flesh-and-blood murderer, but what they overlook is the disappearance of blood from the victims. No ordinary murderer could do *that* — So, of course, the Yard hasn't got anywhere. And won't, as long as it relies on material foundations.'

'Haven't you any ideas yourself, doctor?'

Elsie asked quietly.

'One or two.' He looked at her pensively. 'I've been wondering who in the local cemetery is a suicide — the first necessity for a vampire — and who hated the village people enough to wish to attack them so constantly. I can think of only one person.'

Elsie, her mother, and Peter waited expectantly.

'George Timperley,' Meadows said finally. 'Your late husband, Elsie.'

The girl's expression changed. 'But George *wasn't* a suicide! He died of — myocarditis, or something. Or so you said on the death certificate.'

Meadows smiled faintly. 'Technically, he *did* die of myocarditis, which is only another name for heart-failure. But he was basically a suicide. But for his excessive drinking — my warnings about which he ignored — he would *not* have died. So, I class him as a suicide. As for his hatred of the village folk: we all know that he loathed them. They whispered and talked about his drinking, about the way he treated you . . . '

'Are you seriously suggesting that George became a vampire?' Mrs. Burrows asked blankly.

'I am. He was evil enough, in all conscience . . . ' Meadows moved from the table and came over to where Peter and Elsie were seated on the divan, Mrs. Burrows opposite them.

'I think,' Meadows continued, 'we are facing something dark, something diabolical, and I just can't help linking it with that mystic's warning to you, Elsie.'

'Oh . . . that.' Elsie's mouth tightened a little. 'I have been trying my utmost to forget it. Now I look back on it I think it was crazy; or at least I keep telling myself so.'

'If my guess is right,' Meadows said slowly, 'you, my dear, are the one person whom George, in his present state as a vampire, will seek. He knew you despised him even though you stuck to him: he knew you remained beside him only for what would come to you when he died.'

'Perhaps . . . ' Elsie muttered.

'He *did*. He told me so himself one day when he called for treatment, after too many nights on the bottle. I think he would have changed his will, too, only he died too abruptly to manage it. Just before his death, Elsie, he had guessed at last just how much you really hated him. Hatred, I would remark, is the motivating force which turns a dead being into a vampire, which makes it leave its resting place and, in the form of a bloodsucker, seek out those on whom it desires revenge, turning them in turn into vampires.'

'For heavens' sake, Doc, take it easy!' Peter protested,

'I would be doing a disservice if I did,' Meadows said, shaking his head. 'If the vampire is really George, Elsie, then your life is in danger: it might be George who will make the warning of that mystic come true.'

Elsie gave a troubled frown. 'If it be George why have I not been attacked before now? I don't mean whilst Peter and I were away, of course: I mean before that, after the first attack on Madge Paignton. Nothing has happened to me so far.'

'You are quite a distance from the cemetery in this house,' Meadows answered. 'A vampire cannot go very far without sustenance. In each case attacks have been made on people either within, or just outside, the cemetery. My guess is that, as yet, George has not enough strength to reach you. He might need to kill at least three people in one night, withdrawing their blood into himself, before having sufficient energy to come this far and deal with you.'

'Then — what do we do?' Elsie asked helplessly.

'I would suggest you leave this district. Go as far away as you can, even to another country if possible. Then you ought to be safe. It can't be guaranteed, of course, but it is most probable.'

'And if it *isn't* George,' Peter pointed out, 'we have run away from nothing. I will have left my business, which is now building up into something worthwhile, and Elsie will have left this home — in which we both have ownership now, by the way.'

'Up to you,' Meadows said, shrugging.

'Just a warning, that's all — rendered all the more emphatic by Singh's forecast.'

'Isn't there some way of proving whether or not this vampire *is* George?' Elsie asked slowly.

'Only one. Open his grave and find out.'

'We'd never get permission,' Peter said, rising to his feet. 'And in spite of your own belief in this vampire business, Doc, I still think it's a lot of rubbish! I also think Elsie is in no more danger than you or I. Last of all, I do *not* believe what Rawnee Singh said.'

'I wish I felt the same,' Meadows said. 'As far as George is concerned, the only way to open his grave is to do it ourselves. Certainly the Home Secretary won't agree to exhumation on the basis of vampires. The Government, like Scotland Yard, is singularly unimaginative in regard to matters of the-other world.'

'It's desecration,' Mrs. Burrows whispered. 'You ought to be ashamed of yourself, doctor!'

'I am thinking of the living,' he answered. 'I'm thinking of the possible danger to Elsie. If George is *not* in his grave we know what to think. He has become a vampire. If we attempt to open his coffin it will be at night, when he too will presumably be on the rampage, and his coffin should be empty. By day it will be empty too, he being in a state of suspended animation.'

'I'm not attempting anything so — so horrible,' Elsie said at last. 'I'm staying right where I am, and I'll live down my fears.'

'No more than I expected from you, my dear,' Meadows smiled, patting her shoulder. 'Well, let us hope everything will work out for the best . . . Now I must be going. And keep on with that prescription, Mrs. Burrows.'

She did not answer. Apparently his grave opening suggestion had revolted her completely; so with a nod to Elsie and Peter he picked up his bag and headed for the door.

'I'll see you out,' Peter said, and followed him into the hall. On the front doorstep Peter laid a hand on Meadows' arm.

'Yes?' Meadows asked, putting on his hat.

Peter glanced about him — back towards the drawing room, then on to the darkness of the driveway where Meadows' car stood.

'For Elsie's sake, doc,' he said, his voice low, 'I'd like to satisfy myself about George. I still don't believe in vampires, but if there *is* danger for her — You know what I mean?'

'You mean you're willing to open his coffin?'

'For the sake of Elsie, yes. If George *has* gone, then I must see to it that Elsie leaves the district, and I'll go too, of course.'

Meadows glanced at his watch, then at the night sky.

'Seven-thirty.' he said. 'The night looks as though it ought to be fine, and there's a full moon rising at quarter-to-ten. Tell you what you do. Meet me at the cemetery gates at midnight. Naturally you don't want Elsie to know what you're doing?'

'No. I'll see we get off to bed early, then

I'll sneak out without her being any the wiser.'

Meadows fished inside his overcoat pocket and brought a capsule into view. From it he shook three tablets into his palm and handed them over.

'See these get into her last drink, tonight,' he said. 'Harmless enough, but they'll ensure she doesn't wake until morning. And they won't leave a hang-over, either.'

Peter looked at them. 'Something new in sleeping tablets, eh?'

'Exactly.' Meadows gave a smile. 'I spend quite a lot of my spare time, what there is of it, creating new drugs and cures. Some of them are in fair demand on the market; others are plain failures ... The only way a country doctor can ever hope to add to his finances, I'm afraid. These sleeping tablets are the only ones that produce healthy sleep without any after-effect. I've invented a new form of blood-capsule, too. Restores anaemics to full health, and cures all — or most — other blood diseases. I base my hopes of a fortune on my blood-capsule

. . . Anyhow, I'll be talking shop all night if I'm not careful. See you midnight.'

'Sure enough,' Peter agreed, shaking hands; then when the doctor's car had started off down the drive Peter shut the front door and returned to the drawing room.

'What kept you so long?' Elsie enquired, glancing up from the divan — and breaking off conversation with her mother.

'Oh, nothing. Just talking shop — all about sleeping tablets and blood capsules. The doc's quite a manufacturer of patent medicines, it seems.'

'It's to be hoped some of them are better than this indigestion prescription he's made up,' Mrs. Burrows remarked sourly. 'It doesn't seem to be doing me a bit of good.'

Peter smiled a little and then settled at Elsie's side on the divan. His hand under her chin forced her to look at him. Her blue eyes were half serious, half wistful.

'Still worrying, dearest, deep down?' he murmured.

She sighed. 'Dr. Meadows brought it all back again. I had almost forgotten that horrible warning of death: now I just can't do anything but think about it. Peter, do you think that perhaps the doc was right? About George . . . '

'I think we'd both be more sensible to forget all about the horrible business,' Peter answered. 'Best thing we can do is sleep on it.'

And here he deliberately dropped the subject. He saw to it that the three pills Meadows had given him found their way into Elsie's bedtime drink, and he noticed too that she fell asleep almost at the moment her head touched the pillow. He waited until eleven-thirty to be sure, but she did not stir; then he silently slipped out of the bed, dressed, armed himself with a torch, and left the house by a corridor window. Of Mrs. Burrows he had no fear. Nothing short of an earthquake had ever been known to awaken her, and in any case her room was at the far end of the passage.

For caution's sake, however, Peter did not use his car in case the engine was heard. He walked the distance to the cemetery, striding out swiftly in the pallid

light of the full moon, the still wintry
trees motionless at either side of the lane
leading to the village.

At twelve-fifteen he reached the cemetery gates, to find Dr. Meadows' car parked
there without lights. Meadows himself was
waiting, a bag of tools in one hand and
two shovels over his right shoulder.

'Everything all right?' he enquired.

'Yes — Elsie's none the wiser, and her
mother's sound asleep.'

'Good. I think we'll get into the
cemetery by that twisted railing. Easier
than climbing with all this stuff.' Meadows started walking. 'I've got a crowbar,
screwdriver, torch, the two shovels, and
some rope. And other odds and ends we
may need. We ought to manage all right.'

'You know where George's grave is, of
course?'

'On the right of the church. I was
present when they put him down.'

Peter nodded in the moonlight and said
no more for a while; then when they had
found their way into the cemetery
precincts via the broken railing he
remarked:

61

'This moonlight is going to show us up pretty clearly if anybody happens to be prowling.'

'I know — but it also helps us to see what we're doing. We will have to risk being spotted. Not that I think we will be. The talk of vampires has scared everybody away from here — including Scotland Yard, apparently.'

So Peter did not pursue the subject. They reached George Timperley's grave in another five minutes, identified it by the stone, and then began the task of removing the granite chippings from the topsoil. They worked hard, and in silence, their breath hanging on the still, frosty air. Now and again they paused to look about them, but nothing stirred in the expanse of the burial ground.

Until at last Peter's shovel struck something with a soggy thud. With his hands he pushed away the soil and revealed the still comparatively new oak of George Timperley's coffin.

'This is it,' he murmured, as Meadows crouched beside him. 'Still think we should go through with it?'

'Definitely! That's what we came for.'

The remaining soil was brushed to one side so that the lid with its brass nameplate became revealed. From his bag Dr. Meadows took two screwdrivers, handing one to Peter.

'Better unscrew it instead of using the crowbar,' he said. 'We'll have to screw it up again when we've finished. We'll only use the bar if the screws are too tough.'

Peter nodded and began his task. He did not enjoy one minute of it. As each screw finally succumbed to pressure he began to wonder what would be revealed when the lid was removed. He kept picturing the inroads which decomposition might have made on George Timperley's body. After all, he had been buried for some months, now —

With a protesting squeak the final screws came out and the lid was ready for moving. Peter and Meadows exchanged glances as they stood deep in the grave.

'Ready?' Meadows asked quietly.

'Go ahead. I can stand it if you can.'

Meadows gripped his end of the lid, hesitated for a moment, and then heaved it to one side. Fixedly he stared into the coffin. After a second or two Peter brought himself to looking also. He gave a little gasp.

The coffin was empty.

For a moment or two neither man spoke. There was the moonlight, leprous and cold, glowing down into the grave-pit and clearly revealing the empty box. Peter gave a little shiver, and it was not the frostiness in the air, either.

'You were right, Doc,' he whispered at last.

'I begin to think I — ' Meadows broke off, so suddenly that Peter looked at him in surprise. He found him staring fixedly upwards at the edge of the grave-pit. Peter looked too, and his mind reeled for a moment with sheer incredulity. George Timperley was standing on the edge of the grave, looking down at them. He was in the shroud of death from neck to ankles. His feet, just visible above the piled-up soil, were bare. His arms were motionless at his sides.

'Great God,' Meadows whispered, feeling for the crowbar in the bag beside him. 'It's — it's he! George! We — '

He got no further. Suddenly George Timperley flew into whirlwind action. With a tremendous jump he landed in the grave, his hands clutching savagely about Dr. Meadows' neck. Catching his foot, Meadows stumbled backwards and into the coffin, then he was fighting for his life as Timperley's bared teeth made frantic efforts to get at his throat.

Then Peter attacked. He could not reach the crowbar so he stabbed hard with his screwdriver — or at least intended to do so. Instead Timperley anticipated him, swung round, and lunged out with his white, deadly cold hands. Peter struggled frantically, realizing he was fighting something of superhuman strength. He was borne down onto the coffin edge, his back nearly cracking under the pressure. Everywhere his hands clawed and pulled he felt cold, flabby flesh without a spark of living warmth. The very feel of it turned his stomach inside-out.

Then he saw Timperley's teeth. They were not the teeth he had possessed in life — those even rows in a fairly handsome face. Every one was fanged ,and extra long, like those of a tiger. They snarled and snapped close to his face and the breath of the attacker was like something from a sewer.

Battling and struggling uselessly Peter tumbled fully back into the coffin, then his hair was seized and his head hammered relentlessly on the coffin bottom until his senses spun crazily in darkness . . .

He drifted back to consciousness only slowly, aware of the bitter after-taste of brandy in his mouth. Opening his eyes he recognized Dr. Meadows against the glow of the moon. He put away a flask and breathed heavily.

'Good,' he whispered. 'I'm glad I brought you round . . . '

Peter fingered his throat gently, but apparently it was unhurt. His head ached abominably and he was laid nearly full length in the coffin. With Meadows' help he sat up and his head swam viciously.

'What — what happened to George?' he asked shakily.

'I thrust a Crucifix in front of his eyes.

That did it. I remembered reading somewhere that a vampire cannot face a crucifix — the exact antithesis of itself — so I brought one with me just in case. He flew — literally — out of this grave and I haven't seen him since.'

Peter struggled to his feet. 'Thank heaven for your foresight, Doc,' he muttered. 'I certainly don't need any more convincing in regard to vampires: I've seen enough to satisfy me.'

'We'd better get this coffin fastened up again and refill the grave,' Meadows said. 'We've learned all we need to know. You fit enough to get busy?'

'I'll be all right,' Peter acknowledged, holding his throbbing forehead. 'Give me that screwdriver, will you? If I stoop I'm afraid my skull will explode.'

Meadows said nothing. He handed over the screwdriver and then heaved the coffin lid back into position. When it was finally screwed down he and Peter scrambled up out of the grave and began the job of shovelling back the earth. At the end of an hour the task was finished and the granite chippings duly returned as surface covering.

'Now you know the facts what do you propose doing?' Meadows asked, collecting the shovels and the tool bag.

'Have to tell Elsie, of course, and then I suppose we must get away from here.' Peter looked about him moodily in the leprous moonlight. 'The very last thing I wanted, with my garage business nicely built up. Still, we know George is on the rampage so there's nothing else for it. At all costs I have to do all that is humanly possible to prevent Rawnee Singh's forecast coming true.'

'I've been thinking,' Meadows said, as they began moving. 'You might be able to stay just as you are and still ward off George. I mean the Crucifix. It doesn't have to be mine, though you're welcome to it if you want it. As long as you have that for protection you will be safe. A vampire cannot attack where the Cross faces him.'

Peter nodded slowly. 'That might solve the difficulty. I'll have yours, if you don't mind, and give it to Elsie. I haven't one of my own but I can soon buy one.'

Meadows nodded, and when he and Peter had come beyond the cemetery the doctor removed the Crucifix from his pocket and handed it over.

'There it is, Peter, and I pray heaven it will protect you. As far as George is concerned, I must make arrangements with the villagers, the police — and if possible Scotland Yard — to have him captured and slain by a stake through his heart. Tell Elsie as much as you think she should know. Now, shall I give you a lift home?'

'No thanks, Doc. I'll walk. I can do with the fresh air to clear my head up a bit. It's still pretty woolly — See you again. 'Night.'

Peter shook hands, and holding the Crucifix so he could use it instantly if danger threatened he went up the lane in the moonlight, thinking as he went of the ghoulish experience through which he had passed. Somewhere at the back of his mind plain commonsense told him that the episode just could not have been real, then the pain in his head and the Crucifix in his hand convinced him otherwise.

He re-entered the house the way he had left it, via the top landing window. Without a sound he returned to the bedroom, softly closing the door. Then as he turned into the room he stopped dead — The windows were flung wide open and the draperies were writhing gently in the night wind.

Peter hurried forward, to the bed. Elsie was still there, but the whiteness of the pillow was defiled with dark stains. In the slanting moonlight they looked like —

'Elsie!' Peter whispered in horror; then he switched on the bedside lamp. Instantly the dark stains became red.

The girl was lying motionless, her face deathly white, two vivid punctures at either side of her throat from which trickles of blood had come. It appeared to have dried now.

'*Elsie!*' Peter screamed, and seized her shoulders. But for all his efforts she did not awaken. At last he lowered her back to the pillow and listened for her heart. It was still beating, though somewhat sluggishly.

Peter did not waste any more time. He

rushed from the room, along the landing, then down the stairs into the dark hall. Switching on the lights he whipped up the telephone and rang Dr. Meadows. After a moment or two the tired voice of the medico answered.

'Yes? Meadows here — '

'It's Peter, Doc! Elsie's been attacked by George whilst I was away. At least I suppose it was George. There are two punctures either side of her throat, blood on the pillow, the window open — I can't revive her. She's still alive, but only just I think. For God's sake come over right away, will you?'

'I'll be there,' Meadows promised, his voice taking on more life. 'Keep a watch on her until I arrive.'

Peter put the 'phone down and returned up the stairs. At the top of them he met his mother-in-law, hastily scrambled into a dressing gown, a boudoir cap over her hair-curlers.

'What on earth is going on?' she demanded. 'Peter, what are you doing fully dressed at this hour of the night?'

'Don't bother me now,' Peter answered,

brushing past her. 'Elsie's been attacked by a vampire — probably George. I've just been 'phoning for Dr. Meadows.'

He raced back into the bedroom to find Elsie lying just as he had left her, motionless, hardly breathing, her face as white as the pillow beside it. Mrs. Burrows followed Peter in and stood staring in horror at the defiled pillow and the wounds on her daughter's neck. Then, when the first shock had been absorbed somewhat, she went to the windows and closed them.

'Did you say — George?' she demanded, her eyes fixing on Peter as he sat at the bedside watching Elsie intently.

'He's a vampire. Doc. Meadows and I proved it tonight in the cemetery. We were both attacked — '

'But what on earth — ?'

'Oh, stop bothering me!' Peter snapped. 'I've enough on my mind!'

Mrs. Burrows sniffed, then taking a second chair she sat at the other side of the bed and looked at her daughter in silent consternation.

The intolerably long silence was broken

at last by a pounding on the front door. Peter rushed down to open it and came back with the tired Dr. Meadows behind him. Meadows gave a start as he saw the girl, then he got busy with his stethoscope.

'Well?' Peter asked anxiously. 'What's the verdict?'

'He got her, Peter,' Meadows answered slowly, grey worry in his face. 'No half measures about it. Both jugulars have been pierced and she's lost a good deal of blood.'

'I don't see how,' Peter argued. 'Those big bloodstains on the pillow can't be from her; there are only tiny trickles on her neck from those punctures — '

'The pillow stains probably come from George,' Meadows answered. 'Some blood was spilt as he drew it from Elsie. That's a likely happening in a vampire attack — Only one thing to do,' Meadows finished briefly. 'Keep a watch on Elsie night and day. I'll let you have some blood-restorative pills with full directions how to use them. If she is not attacked again she might recover all she has lost — '

'But doesn't this attack make *her* a vampire?'

'That can only happen if she dies — and that we must prevent at all costs. Hop down to the 'phone, Peter, and call Scotland Yard. Give them every detail and ask for the same Inspector who has been working on this case. No use bothering with those two clowns in the village. Hurry it up, man!'

Peter nodded and dived out of the room. Meadows considered the girl for a moment, then he filled a hypodermic syringe and applied the needle to a vein in the inside of Elsie's upper arm.

'What's that for?' Mrs. Burrows asked, watching intently.

'Blood restorative in liquid form,' Meadows answered. 'I can't administer pills until she recovers consciousness.'

'Peter has been telling me that George caused this — that he has become a vampire. Am I supposed to believe that?'

'With your daughter in this condition I don't see how you can do much else,' Meadows retorted.

'I can't believe in vampires, Doctor.

I've lived too long to believe in *any* superstition of that nature. I prefer to think something material — *very* material — attacked my daughter, not the blood-thirsty ghost of her first husband. It simply screams out against all reason.'

'So do poltergeists, phantoms, and evil spirits,' Meadows answered, his voice quieter. 'Yet they exist . . . '

Since Mrs. Burrows did not pursue the subject he too became silent, working with soft wadding on the punctures in the girl's throat. The more he studied them the more troubled his face became. He was considering the problem in silence when Peter returned, a hand to his still aching head.

'I got Scotland Yard,' he said. 'The sergeant-in-charge will get in touch with Chief-Inspector Rushton and he'll be coming up immediately. He's not in his office at this hour, of course — Well, Doc, how's Elsie going on?'

'Done all I can,' Meadows answered, putting a phial of pills on the table. 'She ought to recover consciousness towards morning. Those sleeping tablets you gave her are hindering things, of course: I'd forgotten them. It may be those, more than actual blood loss, which is keeping her unconscious. Anyway, when she recovers, see she gets these pills every six hours. She's not to get up until I say so. And she must be guarded day and night against all possible attacks. You still have that Crucifix? See that she can keep it handy. In an unguarded moment, it might save her.'

'*Day* and night?' Peter repeated. 'Surely no vampire attack by day is possible?'

Meadows gave a sigh. 'No, of course not. I'm getting too tired to think straight. Guard her from sundown to sunrise. During the day she ought to be safe enough.'

He began to pack up his bag; then Mrs. Burrows spoke.

'Why was Elsie given sleeping tablets? She's in no need of them.'

'I did it to keep her quiet whilst I went out to investigate the cemetery,' Peter said. 'And I am *not* going to argue about it! If you hadn't slept like a log you could have probably saved Elsie from being attacked tonight!'

'Oh?' Mrs. Burrows smiled coldly. 'And if you had stayed beside her, as any right-minded husband should, you could have handled the situation yourself. Instead you had to go rushing off to the cemetery on some wildcat excursion.'

'It wasn't wildcat, Mrs. Burrows,' Meadows said deliberately. 'We discovered George had left his coffin: that is proof that he is a vampire.'

'I don't believe it,' Mrs. Burrows said flatly. 'There's something about all this that's peculiar — diabolical, but I do *not* believe an evil spirit comes into it.'

Meadows gave her a look and then shrugged.

'I have to be going,' he said. 'I've had no sleep yet. Do the best you can, Peter, and I'll be here during the day. If the police want me — as I expect they will — they know where to find me. Good night, Mrs. Burrows.'

'Good night,' she answered indifferently, then she got to her feet.

'You can go back to bed if you wish,'

Peter told her, making himself comfortable on the chair. 'I must stay awake somehow to watch Elsie and open the door to the police when they come.'

'I'll do my share,' she decided. 'I'll rest in the drawing room: you can stay here. And the sooner the police come, the better. If ever there was criminal assault and murder disguised as vampire attacks it is *this*!'

She gave another glance towards her silent daughter, tightened her lips, and then went out. The door closed sharply.

4

Killer From The Grave

It was towards eight in the morning when a police car swept into the drive of the Timperley residence. From it there alighted Chief-inspector Rushton and Detective-sergeant Mather, both of them in plain clothes and far too schooled in crime and criminals to believe in vampires. With them also were two uniformed constables, a divisional-surgeon, and a fingerprint expert.

By this time Elsie was conscious again, but her energy was of such a low order she was hardly able to talk. To the Chief-inspector she had little to say. She was not even aware that she *had* been attacked, remembering nothing since falling asleep the previous night.

Peter, worn out from lack of sleep and anxiety, gave the cemetery details and then, a solid constable on guard, he went to bed. The Chief-inspector picked up the story from that point and the Divisional-surgeon and fingerprint man went to work on their respective jobs.

Rushton, who had handled the earlier business of the two vampire victims, was once again ill-at-ease in investigating this new onslaught. Throughout the day he covered a good deal of ground, questioning Mrs. Burrows, Dr. Meadows, and then several villagers. The coffin of George Timperley was reopened and found to be still empty. The grounds of the cemetery were gone over; and those of the Timperley home. Nothing was left undone, until finally by eight in the evening Rushton returned with his sergeant to the Timperley home to report progress. Because of the necessity of Elsie having to be guarded whilst she lay in bed, he told his story in the bedroom, Peter, Mrs. Burrows, and Dr. Meadows also being present.

'I am quite sure of one thing.' Rushton said, his square face grim. 'The Assistant-Commissioner is going to haul me over the coals when I have to report failure in this business — for the third time.'

'So you've not got anywhere?' Peter asked bitterly.

'I'm afraid not. Fingerprint experts have not found any prints anywhere — or at least any prints that might be of use. What prints there are, chiefly on the window frame of this room here, are blurred with none of the familiar whorl, arch, or loop formation. From the doctor we have the assurance that the blood found on the pillow was yours, Mrs. Malden, which means you actually must have lost far more than that caused by the wounds in your throat. Anyway, the group matches. True, you are not the only person with an 'O' type blood-group, but the coincidence of the attacker losing that much blood, and being in the same group, is *too* coincidental.'

'A vampire is not a creature of flesh and blood, anyway,' Meadows put in. 'Not in the accepted sense, anyhow; so the blood on the pillow *could* only belong to Mrs. Malden.'

'So it would seem,' Rushton admitted. 'We have also made routine enquiries but have got no further than talk of vampires in general and George Timperley in particular. We have not been able to pick up any clues in the cemetery, even though we have noted that George Timperley's grave, or at least his coffin, is empty. We could of course have kept a vigil by night and see if he appears, but you people have already done that and met with no success. So,' Rushton finished. 'I'm afraid we haven't got very far.'

'Not a very encouraging admission for Scotland Yard,' Dr. Meadows commented.

'We're not magicians, doctor,' the Chief-inspector told him. 'In this particular case we are up against a complex problem. A vampire — if such a thing really does exist — is a long way from our territory.'

'Have you thought of the possibility of the vampire being an excuse for some criminally-minded person to commit murder and assault at random?' Mrs. Burrows asked. 'Making everything look as though it is the work of a vampire . . . '

'Yes, we have considered that possibility,' Rushton admitted, 'but it does not get us any further. If it be a tenable theory, the answer is a maniac — and not a sex-maniac, either, since men have been killed as well as women attacked. The whole thing is so motiveless, so utterly lacking in purpose — '

'From a material, standpoint, yes,' Meadows said. 'From the standpoint of a vampire everything fits in. It all comes down to one thing: George Timperley is anxious to destroy his former wife and turn her into a vampire like himself. To do that he needs human blood, so to obtain it he kills off villagers, none of whom he liked whilst he lived. It's as simple as that.'

'And you think Mrs. Malden is likely to be attacked again?' Rushton asked, thinking.

'I am convinced George Timperley will do his best. It is up to us to see that he fails. I think we should organize a vampire-watch amongst the villagers and attack him the next time he appears.'

'It seems to be the only move,' Rushton

agreed, then he switched the subject. 'Tell me, about this mystic, Rawnee Singh. What exactly did he have to say? Do you feel able to detail the facts to me, Mrs. Malden?'

Elsie nodded from where she lay in bed and, by degrees, gave all the details, Sergeant Mather writing busily in his notebook.

'Quite extraordinary,' Rushton said at length. 'I am wondering, since Singh appears to have some kind of other-world connection, whether he might not be able to throw some light on this vampire business.'

'Hardly likely,' Meadows said. 'He's a mystic, and nothing more. Vampires will hardly be in his line.'

'Just the same I think I'll have a word with him,' Rushton decided, getting to his feet. 'He has left this district now, of course, but we can soon trace him — and will. I'll get in touch with you again when I've interviewed him.'

He turned to leave, the Detective-sergeant beside him, then Mrs. Burrows' voice gave them pause.

'Inspector, there's something I'd like to know. What was your divisional surgeon's opinion of the wounds my daughter had sustained?'

'The punctures in her neck, madam? Apparently caused by some lance-like object — which we can only assume were the teeth of the vampire. After that, presumably, your daughter's blood was sucked from the jugular veins. Some of it was spilt in the process, on to the pillow.'

Peter put a hand to his eyes as if to shut out the Chief-inspector's cold matter-of-factness.

'Suppose something had been used to duplicate a vampire's teeth?' Mrs. Burrows persisted. 'Would your surgeon know the difference?'

'I doubt it. In fact he has no more experience of a vampire than I have. He can only assume.'

'Which is what I object to!' Mrs. Burrows snapped. 'There is too much assumption in this business. I believe — '

'Mother, please!' Elsie entreated. 'I can't stand all this noise and argument.'

'No, my dear, of course you can't,' Dr.

Meadows murmured. 'We'll drop the subject, and leave it to you to do what you can, Inspector. At this end we will do our best, also.'

Rushton nodded, bade farewell all round, and then departed with the sergeant beside him. Dr. Meadows considered Elsie for a moment in the light of the bedside lamp, then he glanced at Peter.

'Want me to take it in turns with you to stay on guard?' he asked. 'Hard work for one man alone, and it's hardly a task for you, Mrs. Burrows.'

'Why isn't it?' she asked coldly. 'I've helped all I can up to now.'

'No doubt, but if George Timperley should reappear I very much doubt your ability to deal with him.'

'I'd be glad of your help, Doc,' Peter said. 'If you could take on until about midnight I could grab a few hours' sleep.'

'Gladly,' Meadows assented.

'Which means I am not wanted?' Mrs. Burrows asked.

'Oh, mother, why do you have to be so unpleasant?' Elsie asked wearily. 'Peter and the doctor are only doing what they think is best.'

'When a mother cannot watch over her own child things have come to a nice pass,' Mrs. Burrows retorted. 'At least I know when I'm not wanted.'

She left the room impatiently and was not at all careful about the force with which she closed the door. Since it was still only early in the evening she went down into the drawing room. Switching on the lights she moved to an armchair by the fire and settled down. She did not read, or watch television. She gave herself entirely up to thought.

The longer she was preoccupied the more the lines hardened in her face.

'That could be it,' she told herself at length. 'And it is only right that Inspector Rushton should know what I think. Nothing must be — '

She broke off as there was a sudden click from somewhere. Puzzled, she looked about her, but failed to detect anything unusual. Since it was not repeated she turned back to her thought-ful contemplation of the fire — then with a sudden whirlwind twisting of drapes the French windows burst apart and an apparition in snow white entered.

Mrs. Burrows stared at the visitor blankly. She was too strong-nerved, too self-possessed, to be afraid: she was instead completely bewildered. Fixedly she gazed at the expressionless face. The only part about it that lived were the eyes and the ghastly mouth, besmeared with red about the lips, the fanged teeth bared.

'George Timperley!' she gasped at last, and half got to her feet.

Before she could complete the action the apparition moved forward soundlessly on naked feet. Without him uttering a word, George Timperley's pale, deadly cold hands lashed forward, seizing the now startled Mrs. Burrows by the throat. She managed to give one desperate scream, then she was crushed down again into the armchair.

Tremendous strength held her there. She kicked and lashed furiously, striking at the icy limbs, slapping at flesh that was as cold and revolting as that of a corpse — but she had not the power to prevent that terrifying face with its blood-stained teeth and lips coming ever nearer to her. At last she felt sharp pain at both sides of her neck and could smell the fetid breath of the monster that had come from the grave.

Her struggles grew weaker and at last eased altogether, whilst, upstairs, Dr. Meadows gave Elsie a sharp glance. She lay reading, or trying to, but she lowered the book as his eyes met hers.

'Did you hear something?' he asked, puzzled.

'I heard a cry — or I thought I did,' Elsie responded. 'I don't suppose it was anything, though. Night bird perhaps.'

'Not at this time of year,' Meadows answered. 'I'll awaken Peter and he can watch you whilst I see if all's well.'

He went over to the deep armchair at the far end of the big bedroom, shook Peter into wakefulness and explained matters, and then hurried out of the room. In perhaps three minutes he was back, white-faced and drawn. He closed the door and stood with his eyes shut for a moment as though to blot out something horrifying.

'What?' Peter whispered, and Elsie half rose on her elbow and then sank back again helplessly.

'You'd better — go and look,' Meadows said, getting control of himself. 'It was never more vital for one of us to watch Elsie. Ring the police. They may still be at the inn in the village.'

Peter went out quickly. Elsie watched Meadows anxiously.

'What is it, doctor?' she entreated. 'Tell me: what's *wrong*?'

He came forward slowly to the bedside, looking down at her.

'I have to be brutal, my dear,' he said, taking her limp hand in his fingers. 'You might as well hear the truth now as later . . . Your mother has been murdered. Foully! And George was her killer.'

Elsie moved her lips but no words came forth. Shock had momentarily killed the power of speech.

'I saw George down there,' Meadows continued. 'He was just at the end of — his orgy. He did not stay to attack me, perhaps remembering the Crucifix I 'thrust before his eyes last night.'

'Mother — dead,' Elsie said at last. 'Murdered by — George — I — I just can't believe it! I . . . '

She stumbled over her words, her eyes half closing. Meadows put an arm behind her shoulders and raised her slightly. From the table he took up the blood-capsule phial and pushed off the stopper one-handedly.

'Here, take these,' he murmured, putting three of the pills to the girl's clenched lips. 'They'll help you . . . '

With an effort she opened her mouth and allowed the pills to roll under her tongue, where they dissolved. Then she sank back, her eyes brimming with tears and her shoulders quivering. What happened after that she did not know. Reaction, and the unending horror which seemed to beset her, overwhelmed her.

When she emerged from the coma that seemed to have struck her she learned that a whole fortnight had passed. Her mother had been buried; the police had investigated again and got no more evidence than before; and she herself was suffering from some form of wasting that had no medical explanation.

It was Peter who told her these things, seated at her bedside. Through the window the mid-March sun was shining brightly. The plane trees were just visible, rich with sticky buds, and beyond them again the countryside was preparing for summer.

'If only I could understand it all,' Peter muttered, his face haggard from endless days and nights of worry and watching over Elsie. 'If only I could gauge the depth of George Timperley's hatred of you. If only . . .'

He stopped, sighing, looking at Elsie's white face against the pillow. Always ethereal, even when in the best of health, she looked almost like a ghost now.

'Where's Dr. Meadows?' she asked, her voice so low that Peter had to incline his head to hear her.

'Busy with his practice. He's been grand through these weeks, dearest. Watching over you when I could not, helping in every possible way. He's seen to it that you've been fed by injections whilst you were unconscious. Our job now is to build you up. I've also asked Meadows for another doctor to come and have a look at you. He's a specialist, so maybe he can discover the cause of your slow decline. Meadows can't understand it — from the medical point of view. From the standpoint of the supernatural, though, he says that you have been more seriously bitten than he thought on that night George attacked you. Venom in your blood may be the cause of your . . . illness.'

Elsie said nothing. She looked towards the window, at the glancing sun on the leaves.

'So beautiful out there,' she whispered. 'If only I could go into the garden. You and I together, Peter. If we could walk through the fields, smell the grass, feel the fresh sweet wind of heaven in our faces . . . Rawnee Singh was right, Peter, wasn't he?'

'I still don't believe it,' he answered stubbornly. 'Now you are conscious again we'll get you round. You'll be back to health in no time.'

Elsie shook her blonde head slowly. 'No. Peter. It is not to be. I'm dying . . . I know I am.'

Peter got to his feet. 'I'm going to ring up Meadows. If he isn't home the maid can tell him to come up immediately. I want to know what is to be done now you've come out of your coma — '

'No, Peter — don't leave me.' Her cold, gentle hand caught at his as he turned to go. 'I — I want you to stay.'

'But dearest, I have to look after you. I can't stay here and talk. I want to tell the cook to get something ready for you — '

'Cook? When did we get a cook?'

'Well, she's a sort of housekeeper, cook, maid, and all the lot. I had to get somebody, after your mother went . . . ' Then Peter hurried on, 'I'm sure we'll get results soon. All the village is on the watch for George now. The story is even in the papers under the heading 'The Little Payling Horror.' All kinds of people keep arriving to investigate — Psychic experts, ghost hunters, sightseers. George has made the place famous — '

'You mean infamous,' Elsie whispered.

Then after a long pause she asked, 'Did the Inspector ever find Rawnee Singh again?'

'Yes. But all Singh could do was repeat his statement, just as he had told it to you — and me. As for trying to help the vampire situation, he said it was a manifestation of the dark arts and he would not touch it.'

'How right he was,' Elsie murmured, her eyes closing. 'How terribly, frighteningly right . . .'

Peter looked at her in fear for a moment. She was so utterly still he thought she — Then he gave a smile of relief. Her breast was rising and falling gently. She had merely fallen asleep.

He gently moved his hand away and crept from the room; then he hurried downstairs to the telephone. To his satisfaction Dr. Meadows was at home, having just arrived back from his morning round.

'So she's returned to consciousness?' he asked eagerly, as Peter finished explaining. 'Good! See that she has some nourishing soup to begin with. I'll be over to work things out. Expect me in about twenty minutes.'

Peter rang off and went into the kitchen. Then he returned to the bedroom and crept in silently. Elsie was still sleeping, so quietly she looked almost dead.

She had not awakened by the time Dr. Meadows had arrived. He studied her for a while and then shook his head slowly.

'I don't like it,' he whispered, as Peter stood beside him. 'She's so thin she's nearly a shadow. In the past two weeks she's wasted away in the most alarming fashion — '

'But she can be built up again now she's out of that coma!' Peter looked at him with desperate eyes. 'Doc, we've got to bring her back. I can't bear to think that I might — lose her.'

'We'll do our best, but it's going to be tough. The trouble is, she doesn't answer to any known treatment, which is why I think venom from George when he attacked her is consuming her blood-stream — Oh, I got that other specialist to come. Sir Gerald Montrose. He should be here today.'

'You think he's a good man?' Peter asked.

'I'm convinced of it. I would hardly call on him — thereby admitting myself baffled — if I didn't believe in him. You've heard of him, surely?'

'Afraid not — but you know what you're doing.'

Meadows was silent for a moment, then he pulled up a chair and sat down.

'All we can do is wait for her to awaken again,' he said. 'I wish I'd been here when she awakened before: I could probably have kept her conscious. It may be a long job now.'

'How about your own patients?'

'They can wait. Elsie means more to me than anything else. You know that. She's yours, yes, but that doesn't stop me loving her as much as you do.'

Peter nodded slowly, a thought crossing his mind like a shadow. Then it passed on and he pulled up a chair.

At the end of half an hour Elsie had not awakened. Then the weary waiting was interrupted, by a hammering on the front door. Peter left the room, but evidently the housekeeper had already got ahead of him.

'Who is it, Mrs. Dawlish?' he asked, from the head of the stairs.

'It's a Mr. Rawnee Singh, sir. He says he would like to see you.'

'Singh!' Peter gave a start. He glanced back towards the bedroom, hesitated, and then made up his mind. Quickly he hurried downstairs into the hall. He found Mrs. Dawlish regarding the brown-skinned visitor in some suspicion.

'All right, Mrs. Dawlish, thank you,' Peter said to her. 'I'll attend to Mr. Singh.'

Mrs. Dawlish bustled away and Peter looked at the mystic in surprise.

'What brings you here, Mr. Singh? I thought you'd dropped right out of sight.'

'An interview I had with Chief-inspector Rushton led me to examine the case of your wife again, Mr. Malden. I had the idea you might wish to hear my conclusions.'

Peter said nothing. He opened the drawing room door and led the way into it. Then he motioned Singh to a chair. He sat down with a cat-like elegance, his eyes intently studying Peter's face. Even here, with modern furniture around him, his manner was still that of the enigmatic Easterner, rendered all the more obvious by his silk turban with a small jewel in its centre.

'I have little time to spare, Mr. Singh,' Peter said quietly. 'I don't wish to seem rude, but my wife is desperately ill and I am keeping a constant watch on her — '

'Along with Dr. Meadows. Yes, I know.' Singh gave his faint smile. 'I am afraid both of you are wasting your time. It is willed that your wife will die, Mr. Malden — only much sooner than I had thought. That is what I came to tell you. After Inspector Rushton questioned me and I realized that your wife was surrounded by an aura of dark evil I made a special point of studying her vibrations. I found that she will die — today. I thought that if I came personally and told you this you would not find it such a terrible shock when her life ceases.'

'I don't believe it,' Peter said obstinately.

'You mean you prefer not to,' Singh corrected. 'It is no use, Mr. Malden: you cannot defeat destiny . . . However, I also looked further and I discovered that your wife's death is, actually, only the beginning of a new life for her — '

'So you're going to start preaching about the Hereafter as well?' Peter demanded, his nerves on edge. 'I'm in no mood to listen.'

'You misunderstand me. I mean that your wife will start life anew as a vampire. That, too, would have come as a terrible shock had I not arrived to warn you.'

Peter sat down slowly. He found it impossible to push Singh's statements on one side: there was too much solemn conviction about them.

'Mr. Singh,' he said deliberately, 'you once said you had sympathetic feelings towards people. Is there nothing you can do to help us? You read the future — accurately it would appear. Is there nothing that can be done to save my dear wife from the fate hovering over her?'

'I am afraid not . . . ' Singh considered for a moment, then a thoughtful look crossed his brown features. 'There is something,' he said finally, 'which is not quite *right* about this whole business.'

Peter laughed hollowly. 'Not quite right? The whole thing smells of diabolical evil from start to finish.'

'I did not quite mean it in that sense,' the mystic said. 'I am referring to the underlying current in your wife's aura. I think I should explain that I read the future by means of the vibrations given off by a living body. I believe that these vibrations exist as a pattern and foretell the destiny of a living creature from the cradle to the grave. Normally, the cessation of these vibrations represents death — but in certain abnormal cases it could, I suppose, also represent a cessation of bodily functions.'

'Like unconsciousness?' Peter suggested.

'Something more than that. Unconsciousness alone does not prevent bodily vibrations being given off, just as an unconscious person still breathes. No, I mean something more. Let us say — suspended animation. A state wherein

101

the body seems to be dead, but is not.'

Peter got to his feet again and paced around the room slowly, thumb and finger to his eyes.

'Too confusing for me, Singh,' he said finally. 'Just what are you getting at?'

'I am wondering,' Singh mused, 'if I have really foreseen death, or something else. Your wife's existence is certainly going to pass through an eclipse — that is inevitable — but I know she will reappear alive, as a vampire — after she has been buried. There is something about it all which is not — absolute.' Singh moved worriedly.

'Death should bring finality. Her change into a vampire should not become *apparent* to me because a vampire is outside the realm of human vibrations. Yet I see it . . . '

Peter came to a stop, a thought turning over in his mind. Before he could utter it a shout from the top of the stairs sent him hurrying into the hall. Meadows was at the stair top.

'Better come, Peter,' he said anxiously. Forgetting all about Singh — and everything else — Peter dived for the staircase and sped up it. At the summit Meadows caught his arm.

'Just a minute, son,' he murmured. 'I'm afraid — it's all over. She died a few minutes ago.'

Peter stood motionless for a moment, the colour leaving his face; then he turned round and raced up to the bedroom. He did not stop hurrying until he reached the bedside, then he caught Elsie's limp hand. It was still warm — but lifeless. Through eyes blurring with tears he gazed at her dead face. It was smiling a little. Wisps of her blonde hair were moving gently in the breeze from the window, which Dr. Meadows had opened.

'Nothing I could do, Peter,' he said. 'She just passed away without regaining consciousness. I wish you'd been here — '

'I was talking to Singh,' Peter said mechanically, and Meadows gave a start of surprise.

'You mean the mystic? What on earth's he doing here?'

'Didn't you hear Mrs. Dawlish call his

name from the hall?' Peter turned weary eyes. 'No — I suppose you wouldn't.'

He looked up as Rawnee Singh himself appeared in the doorway. He hesitated for a moment and then came forward. Impassively he looked at the lifeless girl.

'What do you want here?' Meadows demanded. 'Don't you realize that this is — '

'The living may look upon the dead, doctor,' Singh replied, with a direct stare of his oblique eyes. 'Just as the living may look upon — the living.'

'What are you talking about?' Meadows snapped.

'Death takes many forms,' Singh answered ambiguously. Then he looked at Peter. 'My sincere condolences, Mr. Malden, in your present ordeal. I feel though that the end is not yet. To material eyes — yes. It is the end. The world will say it is death. As for me . . . ' He did not finish. Instead he held out his dark hand. 'For the time being, Mr. Malden, farewell. We shall meet again in the not too distant future. That, too, is pre-destined.'

Peter shook hands mechanically and watched the mystic leave the room silently. Dr. Meadows gazed after him and then looked back at Peter.

'What did he want here?' he demanded.

'He came to tell me of two things, Doc. That Elsie would die today, and that she will become a vampire.'

Meadows' face clouded. 'So George's ambition is to be fulfilled? His attack upon her succeeded, though it has taken some time for her to pass away. If she becomes a vampire, Peter, we have only one course . . . to drive a stake through her heart at her first appearance from the grave.'

Peter said nothing. He drew the sheet over the dead face of the girl and left the room.

5

The Terrible Corpses

At two o'clock Sir Gerald Montrose, the specialist in heart and blood disorders, arrived in his gleaming Buick. He was a small, pink-faced man with flawless manners and hands like a woman's. Since he had arrived too late to help Elsie he could only make a post-mortem examination and pool his diagnosis with that of Dr. Meadows.

Peter, at the end of making funeral arrangements and feeling too stunned to care whether he lived or died, studied the two medicos as they ran him to earth in the drawing room.

'Because of the unusual circumstances surrounding Elsie's death, there'll probably be an inquest,' Dr. Meadows said. 'At any rate I have informed the Local coroner of her death. In the meantime, Sir Gerald and I are both of the same opinion regarding her demise. It was caused by pernicious anaemia — '

'It was caused by a vampire,' Peter interrupted stonily. 'The vampire that was George Timperley. He bit Elsie, sucked away a lot of her blood, and poisoned that which was left.'

'That may be the truth,' Sir Gerald agreed, 'but we have to convince a jury which deals only in facts. A coroner's jury would not accept the vampire angle. Hence we have to state a medical reason for your wife's unhappy death.'

'Do what you like,' Peter muttered, gazing dully in front of him. 'I just don't care what happens any more.'

But the movement of events did not allow Peter to sink into himself. He had to attend the coroner's inquest and the death of Elsie was debated in detail. Rawnee Singh also gave evidence, and Chief-inspector Rushton. The other-world atmosphere of the whole business, however, made it impossible for the hearing to be brought to a logical conclusion, so finally the coroner was compelled to accept the joint opinions of

Sir Gerald Montrose and Dr. Meadows . . .

For Peter, the rest was a nightmare, rendered all the more horrifying by Singh's forecast that, once buried, Elsie would become a vampire. He became haunted by the thought that he would have to join the villagers in a constant watch on Elsie's grave to make sure that, when she did appear, she was slain by a stake through her heart. He began to wonder whether life was worth living at all, whether he might not end it and —

No, that would never do. Besides, he still had the memory of Singh's words. The mystic, for some reason best known to himself, was not entirely convinced by the happenings. It gave Peter the dim hope that somehow, somewhere, there might be an answer to all the frightful things that had happened — an answer in which he, and others, could believe.

The day of the funeral came. Four pallbearers entered the house. Peter watched from the hall. He was dressed in sombre black, his face white and serious. He saw them come downstairs, carrying the coffin — then they took it out to the hearse and slid it gently into position. After that there was some ten minutes of wreath-laying.

Dr. Meadows arrived before the funeral cortège started off. He said but little. There was sorrow deep in his eyes, but it had not the naked hurt expressed in Peter's features ... Mrs. Dawlish was present too, in sombre clothes. The remainder of the mourners were chiefly those few from the village who had ignored malicious gossip and liked Elsie for herself.

So the forlorn journey to the cemetery began. The weather had turned unseasonable. There was a cutting wind and a light, saturating rain. The vicar seemed to mumble the burial service. At the back of the church sat Rawnee Singh, utterly unemotional, listening intently. He was also present at the graveside and watched Peter hurl a handful of earth down into the grave on top of the coffin. Then it was all over and Elsie had been laid to rest — at least so far as human endeavour could plan it. What might happen later nobody, except maybe Singh, knew.

Peter, for his part, had come now to the task he had been fearing the most. He had to make arrangements for a watch to be kept over Elsie's grave. He would probably have shirked it altogether, only Dr. Meadows did not allow him to.

He insisted that a meeting should be held that evening in the main lounge of the village inn — and Peter had to be there whether he liked it or not.

He found the room fairly crowded with villagers, both men and women, when he arrived towards eight o'clock. He waited until Dr. Meadows came, and then explained the situation.

'This, for me, is the most difficult thing I have ever attempted,' he said, with a serious glance at the faces turned towards him. 'I am having to ask for volunteers to strike down my wife — by driving a stake through her heart — if she is seen to leave her grave. We all know that she died because of a vampire attack by her former husband, George Timperley, which makes it inevitable that she will become a vampire in turn. We have already

110

experienced the horror of a vampire in our midst: unless we can take prompt action we are liable to have yet another vampire . . . my wife.'

'It does not follow that she will actually be seen leaving her *grave*,' Dr. Meadows pointed out. 'She will have the power of any spirit to pass through solids and might also have the gift of invisibility until she is about to strike; then invisibility will be useless to her. By this I mean that she may appear anywhere, anytime, either in some part of the cemetery or outside it. It will be by night, not day. We shall have to be always on the alert.'

'Otherwise there'll be more murders?' somebody asked.

'That is inevitable,' Meadows agreed. 'Remember that Mrs. Malden had no reason during life to be friendly towards you villagers. You pilloried her because she married so soon after her first husband's death. Since then you have heard, chiefly at the inquest, how brutally her first husband treated her. You also know how he avenged himself: by destroying her — albeit slowly — and leaving the mark of the vampire upon her.'

'George Timperley — the vampire, that is — hasn't been seen for some time,' a woman remarked. 'What do you suppose has happened to him, doctor?'

For a moment or two Meadows considered this; then he replied:

'It is possible that his only aim in rising from the grave as a vampire was to find his former wife and leave his mark upon her. With that accomplished his foul mission was, perhaps, completed. There is only one way to make sure.'

'Open his grave?' Peter asked.

'Exactly. I think we should do that — tonight if possible. Scotland Yard do not seem to be getting anywhere, and since we in this village are the most likely potential victims for future attack we might as well see how we stand.'

'We can do that when we're in the cemetery tonight,' Peter said. 'I want volunteers who'll agree to keep watch in the cemetery — maybe every night for a month, or until such time as we are satisfied as to what is happening.'

There was no lack of response to his request. Several hands went up, mostly from dour-looking farmers in whom superstition was deep-rooted.

'A dozen,' Peter said, nodding as he counted the hands. 'That's fine. Say six each alternate night. That should be enough. I too will stay on watch alternate nights, commencing tonight.'

'Might I join too?' asked a quiet voice, and Peter looked quickly towards the doorway where a man had just come in. He was wearing a mackintosh and a turban.

'You still around this district, Singh?' Meadows asked him bluntly. 'What do you hope to accomplish now the worst has happened?'

'I have yet to be assured, my dear doctor, that the worst *has* happened . . . ' The mystic came forward with his catlike tread and paused a few feet away from where Peter and Meadows were standing.

'You don't regard the death of my wife as the worst?' Peter demanded bitterly.

'No.' Singh gave him a direct look from his dark eyes. 'I shall consider the worst has happened when your wife reappears as a vampire . . . as she will. I am anxious to see that happen.'

'Why?' Meadows asked.

'Chiefly to satisfy myself that I have read the future aright.'

Singh turned as a burly farmer tapped him on the arm.

'Look here, mister, I don't quite understand where you fit into this business. D'you mean you actually read the future?'

'It is my profession.' Singh agreed, with his inscrutable smile. 'I am able to use my poor gifts to read destiny . . . I knew Mrs. Malden would die. I also know she will reappear as a vampire.'

'Oh, you do!' Grim suspicion crossed the farmer's face. 'You seem to know one hell of a lot! Maybe the police would like a word with you.'

'They've already had one,' Peter said. 'Mr. Singh is a mystic — so he says — and so far everything he has foreseen has come true. Some of you may remember him at the Christmas fair.'

The farmer snapped his fingers. '*That's*

where I've seen you! You told Sam Jenkins that his haystack would catch fire on the night of January 10th, didn't you?'

'I hardly remember . . . Naturally, it *did* catch fire?'

'Yes. We never found out how. Come to think of it, you could have fired it yourself to make a prophecy come true — '

Singh held up his hand. 'Gentlemen, I beg of you not to anger the powers that be by discrediting them. That can only bring disaster on all of us.'

'I think,' Meadows said deliberately, 'you are going to cause a great deal of trouble amongst us, Singh, if you stay in this district.'

'Perhaps I am not alone in that,' he responded. 'In any case I intend to remain. I have a friend just outside the village with whom I'm staying. This business of Mrs. Malden interests me tremendously. Anything with an other-world flavour commands my attention.'

Obviously he was not to be shaken off, so neither Meadows nor Peter took any further notice of him. He joined the party of six who went to the cemetery towards eleven o'clock to keep the first night's vigil. The dismal dreariness of the day had been carried on into the night and drizzle was still descending from a black sky as the party, hurricane lamps swinging, made its way to the new grave where Elsie lay buried. For a moment or two, when the grave had been reached, Peter stood looking at the headstone and the still fresh wreaths: then he turned to Meadows.

'I'll stay here with three men, Doc,' he said. 'You'd better take the opportunity to open up George's grave and see how things are.'

Meadows nodded, signalled to the remaining three men who were carrying shovels and tools, then they went off into the murk. Peter watched them go, then he looked back at the villagers in their rain-soaked mackintoshes. Singh was there too, immobile in the light of the hurricane lamps.

'You don't want to satisfy yourself about George Timperley, then?' Peter asked him.

'My interest is in your wife, Mr. Malden.'

'You mean my *late* wife . . . '

'As you wish. For myself I have still to be satisfied on that point.'

'What do you mean by that?' Peter demanded. 'Can't you see that we're all of us under strain enough — myself in particular — without you making all kinds of enigmatic remarks?'

'I ask your forgiveness,' Singh murmured, with a slight obeisance. 'I was merely thinking it would be more sensible to open your wife's grave than George Timperley's, since it is she with whom we're concerned.'

Peter hesitated and the men with him glanced at each other.

'It is so obvious a course,' Singh added, spreading his hands. 'If her coffin is empty we know that we have to be on the alert. If she still lies there, then — for the time being at least — we have nothing more to guard against.'

'I'll ask the Doc when he comes back,' Peter decided.

'He may be a long time,' Singh remarked, with a glance at the distant spots of light where the hurricane lamps stood by George Timperley's grave. 'I would advise you to dig now. There are tools here — and shovels. I am not averse to doing my share.'

'He may be right, Mr. Malden,' one of the men said. 'It's up to you, though. She's *your* wife — or was.'

Peter spent a further moment or two trying to make up his mind, then before he could do so a scream from the lane which ran past the cemetery made him glance up sharply. Singh, and the three other men, swung round and stared through the drizzle.

The scream came again, choking off into a ghastly shriek.

'Trouble!' Peter snapped. 'Come on — !' He whipped up a shovel as a weapon and started racing along the shale pathway. Meadows and the men working with him had also heard the cries and were heading towards the gap in the cemetery railings when Peter and his party caught up.

In a moment or two the entire group was in the lane, the hurricane lamps swinging, heading towards the lights of the doctor's car from where the scream had seemed to emanate.

They came upon the cause of the trouble abruptly — too abruptly for the good of their nerves. Two men were lying face down in the lane, arms and legs sprawled as grotesquely as though they were rag dolls.

'Sergeant Blair and Constable Hawkins!' Meadows gasped. 'The pair of them!'

He hurried forward, hurricane lamp in hand. Putting it down in the roadway he turned both men over, frowning as he felt how flaccid their bodies were. Peter and the rest of the men, Rawnee Singh in the background, looked down in silent horror on two bodies from which every scrap of blood had apparently been drained. The corpses were dehydrated in some extraordinary way, leaving folds of flesh clinging to the bone structure. And on the throats of both men were deep, vividly stained punctures.

'Well, do I have to explain this?' Meadows asked, looking up at the grim faces in the lamplight. 'Our two stalwart guardians of the law have obviously been attacked and slain by a vampire — either

George Timperley, or . . . '

'Go on, say it!' Peter snapped. 'Or Elsie!'

'I'd sooner you said it for me,' Meadows responded. 'Evidently these two poor devils were set upon as they patrolled the lane out here: They promised they would do, remember, when we told them of our plans for tonight. The point is, *which* vampire caused this ghastly business? Not a drop of blood is left in either man!'

'Only thing for it is for some of you men to transport these terrible corpses back into the village for the Yard men to see tomorrow,' Peter instructed. 'We'll carry out our original idea of opening Elsie's grave.'

'You mean George's,' Meadows corrected, standing up.

'And Elsie's. Mr. Singh thought it would be a good idea; and I agree.'

Peter turned to Singh for confirmation, but the mystic had disappeared.

'Where's he gone?' Peter demanded, looking about him in the dark and drizzle. 'Singh! Where are you?'

There was no response. Meadows gave a shrug.

'Be damned to the man: he's no use to us, anyway. Seems to spend all his time arguing for the wrong side . . . You two men get these bodies back to the village,' he instructed. 'Go and fetch a truck if you have to. The rest of us will go back into the cemetery. We'll open both graves while we're at it.'

Turning, he led the way back down the lane, Peter at his side.

'I'm getting a bit baffled by Singh, Peter,' Meadows said anxiously, after making sure the rest of the party was out of earshot. 'He behaves in such a strange way and seems to know so much he's got me wondering . . . '

'About what?'

Meadows did not answer until the main cemetery path had been regained. Then he said:

'I am wondering if he possessed some strange influence over Elsie, which brought about her death. I am not one who believes in what is called the 'evil eye,' even though I think vampires exist

— but I am commencing to wonder if perhaps, when Elsie visited him that evening at the fair, he did not put some kind of psychic spell upon her. He was so convinced she would die, but he erred in the time, apparently. Doesn't that suggest to you that perhaps he did not really know how long it would be before she succumbed? When he had *really* worked it out he came and made amendments to his calculations.'

'But what on earth reason would he have for wanting to kill Elsie? There's no sense in it! Besides, that doesn't explain away George being a vampire.'

'I suppose not — unless Singh is perhaps accountable for that also, in some way so complex the solution has not yet occurred to us.'

Peter did not pursue the subject because the remainder of the party had caught up, barring the two men who had gone back to the village for transport for the two corpses in the lane.

'I'll join you later,' Meadows said, pausing beside George Timperley's half dug-up grave. 'You'd better see what kind of a tale Elsie's coffin has to tell.'

Peter nodded and went on ahead with three of the men. He did not need to give them instructions. They removed the wreaths reverently and set them on one side; then, Peter handling his shovel with as much vigour as his colleagues, the first moves in the exhumation of Elsie began.

They had just got as far as the lid of her coffin when Meadows appeared at the grave edge with the man who had been helping him.

'It wasn't George,' he said. 'He's returned to his coffin, lying there as if he's never done a wrong thing.'

Peter lowered his shovel and looked up incredulously in the glow of the hurricane lamp.

'You mean — through the soil, the screwed lid, and everything?'

'That isn't remarkable, Peter. A spirit, evil or good, can pass through all solids. It satisfies me that his sole reason for becoming a vampire was to inflict Elsie with his own loathsomeness.'

'Which means it was *she* who attacked

and killed those two policemen tonight?' Peter whispered.

'It looks horribly like it.' Meadows jumped down into the grave. 'How far have you got towards opening her coffin — ? Oh, just got to the lid, eh? All right — carry on.'

Peter did not move. Now he had come to the task of removing the screws from the lid his nerve had failed him. Meadows gave him an understanding smile in the glow of the lamp and picked up a screwdriver, motioning the other men to get their tools from the bag.

Swiftly the lid was unfastened — and raised. There was a long and deathly silence.

'Gone!' Peter breathed, staring at the emptiness. Just the plush, the headrest, the lead lining — that was all. The coffin still smelled of the aromatic ointments the undertakers had used.

'Yes — gone.' Meadows took a deep breath. 'She was only buried this morning. She would not leave her coffin during the daylight hours, and we entered the cemetery at eleven. That means that she started to prowl as a vampire somewhere between darkness and eleven o clock. There were two hours of darkness there when she was unguarded. Fools that we've been! We should have come sooner!'

'It would not have availed you anything if you had.'

Meadows, Peter, and the rest of the men looked up sharply. At the edge of the grave, his queer, oblique eyes peering into the cavity, Rawnee Singh was waiting. With his turban and rain-glistened mackintosh he cut a queer figure against the drizzling dark.

'What the devil are you talking about?' Meadows snapped.

'I mean, my dear doctor, that I was here tonight from sunset to the time when I joined your party.'

'You were?' Peter looked surprised. 'How did that come about?'

'You wish to make a mystery of it? That would be rather pointless, would it not? We finished discussing in the inn at about half past eight. It was just commencing to grow dark then. We had arranged to meet at eleven. I had nothing with which to occupy myself in the intervening time — so I came here.'

'And saw what?' Meadows questioned.

'Nothing. Absolutely nothing. I am prepared to swear by all the gods I hold sacred that this grave — and that of George Timperley — remained undisturbed throughout the time I was here. I stood in the chapel porch over there, where I could see both graves — '

'In the dark?' Peter interrupted.

'It is never entirely dark in an open space, my friend. The departure or entry of the occupant of either grave would have been visible because of the white shroud each would be wearing. There was no such manifestation.'

'We've only your word for it,' Meadows said. 'Personally I'm not at all satisfied with your behaviour, Singh. That you came here by yourself is at least — suspicious.'

'Is it?' Singh gave his slow smile. 'Do you believe that *I* perhaps arranged for Elsie Malden to leave her resting place?'

'Just what *are* we to think?' Peter

demanded. 'The fact remains that Elsie would not leave her grave by daylight. The only time she could have departed was in the interval when you say nothing happened. And those two dead men in the lane are proof that she *must* have become a vampire.'

'You are sure it was not George Timperley?' Singh enquired.

'Certain. He's back in his coffin.'

'Strange,' the mystic mused. 'Very strange.'

'No more strange than your remarks and behaviour,' Meadows said. 'Where have you been during the interval? We lost track of you after those two men were found in the lane.'

There was a queer light in Singh's eyes as he looked down into the grave.

'I busied myself doing something which all of you gentlemen neglected to do. I looked for evidences of the attacker.'

'Evidences?' Peter repeated. 'What need was there for that? Weren't those two blood-drained corpses sufficient evidence in themselves?'

'Not altogether. I had the wish to

discover some sign of the creature, or object, which had so ruthlessly slain them. I was successful. Fortunately the night is wet and footprints are clearly visible. In the clayey soil at the side of the lane, not far from your car, doctor, I found signs of heavy boots. Two sets — one belonging to a smallish man, and the other to a much bigger person.'

This sudden material discovery in the midst of the supernatural gave Peter a decided mental jolt.

He looked up at Singh fixedly.

'Do you mean,' Meadows asked deliberately, 'that you think ordinary human beings attacked those two poor devils?'

'I consider there is that possibility,' Singh replied. 'I expected to find the naked footprints of a woman — but there were none. Only these footprints of two men, going up the bank into the field beyond.'

'And then where?' Peter asked quickly.

'I lost them in the grass,' Singh answered, impassive again.

Dr. Meadows became thoughtful. 'This may throw a new light on things.' he said.

128

'It makes me think of something poor Mrs. Burrows once said — You remember, Peter, when she asked me did I think that perhaps a maniac was at work, making everything look as though a vampire were the cause?'

'I remember,' Peter assented. 'But no human agency could account for Elsie leaving her coffin. And what about George Timperley? He didn't only leave his coffin: he returned to it! I just can't see any criminal being responsible for things like that.'

'On the other hand, spirits do not wear size seven and nine boots,' Singh commented.

'I'd like to see those prints,' Meadows decided. 'We had better return this coffin and grave to normal and then perhaps you won't mind showing me what you've discovered?'

'With pleasure,' Singh murmured, and from there on he did not pass any comment. He assisted in the task of re-closing the grave and when it was done, to the point of the wreaths being back in position, he looked from one man to the other.

'Do you consider, doctor, there is any point in maintaining guard here?' he asked. 'We have proved Mrs. Malden has left her coffin. What more — '

'She has to be found,' Meadows interrupted. 'Two of us must keep on constant watch, being relieved at intervals . . . You two men can stop,' he added, motioning to the couple who had done most of the digging. 'The rest of us will go and see those prints you're talking about, Singh.'

The mystic nodded and led the way from the cemetery. When a point of the lane was reached near Meadows' car Singh pulled a small torch from his pocket and flashed the beam on the wet ground.

After searching for a moment or two he picked up the perfectly clear prints, freshly made, which went up the bank and vanished in the field beyond.

'No doubt about that,' Meadows admitted. 'But they lost themselves in the grass above, didn't you say?'

'Unfortunately, yes.'

There was silence for a moment. Then, after pondering, Meadows turned up his coat irritably against the drizzle.

'Doesn't seem to be much more we can do,' he said. 'You said, Peter, that you were staying on watch tonight. That still go?'

'Definitely,' Peter answered. 'If there's any chance of locating Elsie I don't intend to lose it. If nothing happens you can take over tomorrow night.'

Meadows nodded. 'Very well then . . . There are two men who can help you if anything happens; and you other two,' — he looked at the couple standing beside him — 'had better stay around here in case of trouble. You're taking on the job of those two luckless policemen. Or are you scared to do it?'

The two men shook their heads. Countrymen, both of them, they were not easily frightened.

'Will those two policemen become vampires when they're buried?' Peter asked; and Meadows shrugged.

'Presumably — *if* they were killed by a vampire. From these other evidences Singh has found I am beginning to wonder . . . Can I give you a lift back, Singh?'

'Thank you, no.' The mystic's white teeth gleamed in a smile. 'I have decided to stay. Probably Mr. Malden will be glad of my company.'

'He has the other two men,' Meadows pointed out.

'The more I have the better,' Peter answered. 'You carry on, Doc, and I'll see you tomorrow . . . or rather when the day comes.'

Meadows nodded and walked back to his car. After a while it started off down the lane, the red rear light disappearing in the drizzle. The two countrymen looked at each other, turned their collars up higher, and then began a slow pacing back and forth after the manner of sentries.

'I suppose we'd better get back to the cemetery grounds, Singh,' Peter remarked.

'I think we could turn our time to better purpose, Mr. Malden,' the mystic answered. 'Following those footprints, for example.'

'But I thought you said the trail lost itself in the grass!'

'To a certain extent it does. I did not take the time to examine the traces thoroughly. We can do so now, since those other men are on the watch in the cemetery.'

Peter did not agree immediately. Wandering in an open field in the early hours of the morning, and with only Rawnee Singh for company, seemed to him a dangerous occupation. It was not that he was frightened of the mystic, but he was certainly uneasy about him. Left to his mercy Peter was not sure but that he might suddenly pull a knife.

'You hesitate,' Singh murmured. 'Surely, Mr. Malden, you are anxious to know *everything* about this unhappy, ghoulish business?'

'Of course.' Peter made his decision abruptly. 'We'll see what we can find.'

He scrambled up the bank quickly, Singh following behind him with his torch beam waving. Here at the top of the bank the rain and wind seemed heavier. Peter stood huddled and waiting as the mystic caught up with him, the circle of light flashing on the wet soil to reveal the two sets of prints clearly.

'They both come and go,' Singh pointed out. 'Observe?'

Peter looked with renewed interest. So

far he had only thought of them moving one way — from the lane, but not to it.

'It is my belief,' Singh continued, 'that two men came from somewhere, attacked the unfortunate policemen, and then retreated. The prints going away from the lane are much deeper than those going towards it. Plainly, the men carried something heavy.'

'Not bodies, anyway,' Peter said. 'We found those.'

'Perhaps — blood,' Singh said. 'It would weigh as heavy as water, and there must have been a good deal of it.'

'Now we're back where we started,' Peter sighed. 'You are trying to offer a material explanation for something which we believe my wife — as a vampire — created.'

'Do you *wish* to believe that of your wife?'

'My God, no! I'm simply thinking that — '

'Mr. Malden,' Singh interrupted, 'we have here the first signs which suggest that this business of vampires may not be entirely genuine. Let us see if we can discover the starting point of these prints.'

So there began for both of them the

slow, tedious business of following first one set of prints, and then the other, pushing aside wet grass to find the indentations in the oozing soil below. Foot by foot progress was made until, gradually, out of the murk, there loomed a dark towering shape which Singh's torch beam could just pick out as a crumbled wall gleaming with rain.

'From the look of things, Mr. Malden,' he commented, 'our trail ends and begins there — at that wall.'

'We'd better make sure,' Peter said, satisfied by this time that Singh was evidently not planning any kind of attack.

He hurried forward the few remaining yards, Singh behind him, and they stopped when they had gained the towering ruin. At the base of the wall the prints were still visible. They went through a gap in the wall and vanished again in the stone riddled square that had once been a quadrangle.

'What *is* this place?' Singh questioned, switching off his torch for the moment. 'I am not familiar with the local history.'

'It's the old chapel,' Peter responded. 'About fifteen years ago it was destroyed by fire. This is the only remaining wall. In the square here there used to be the cloisters, and under them several of the crypts and mausoleums. It's a spot with historic connections and that's all. The new chapel in the cemetery was built to replace this one.'

'Interesting,' Singh commented. 'I find it most — Look!' he broke off quickly, and gripped Peter's arm.

Peter gazed steadily, feeling his heart beginning to race. There was no doubt of the fact that at the far end of the ruined cloisters a figure had come into view. In the darkness and rain it was only a blurred grey outline, but as Singh switched on his torch details leapt into view.

It was Elsie, her hair flowing in the wind, the shroud moulded against her graceful form!

6

The Walking Dead

For a moment or two Peter could not believe what he saw, but gradually the penetrating beam of the torch forced him to it. Undeterred by it, apparently, Elsie continued to advance, making no sound, the shroud blowing out behind her in the wind. The effect was eerie in the extreme, her form vanishing at intervals as she passed the crumbled stonework that had once formed part of the cloisters.

'What do we do?' Peter whispered at length.

'Slay her, my friend. We have no alternative. That is our main reason for being here, is it not?'

'I can't do it. I can't even bear to look at her — '

Peter half turned to go but Singh flung out his free hand and stopped him.

'If you have not the courage to kill her,

Mr. Malden, then neither have I. We'll see what happens.'

As though drawn to them by magnetism Elsie finally left the protected area of the old cloisters and stepped into the open quadrangle. Immediately the wind began to buffet her and her shroud became plastered to her slender figure with the rain.

'That's queer,' Peter said, frowning. 'She must have been perfectly dry until she got this far. Where's she been, I wonder — ?'

'Her mouth seems to tell the answer,' Singh muttered; and watching intently as the girl came ever nearer Peter could see what he meant. Her lips were dyed red, far beyond their normal shade.

'I don't believe it,' Peter said stubbornly. 'Elsie would never become a vampire! It's all crazy, insane! I saw her die — I also saw her buried — Yet now she's walking! I've got to know the truth — !'

He suddenly lunged forward and raced across the quadrangle to where she was advancing. Reaching her he seized her slender shoulders fiercely. He had time to notice that they were icy cold through the rain-saturated shroud.

'What in God's name has happened, dearest?' he demanded, halting her.

She looked at him fixedly in the light of Singh's advancing torch as he hurried across the wind-swept space. Peter tried to look only into the dull stare of her eyes. He kept his gaze away from the reddened lips.

'I'm Peter,' he insisted, hugging her to him fiercely. 'For heaven's sake, Elsie, speak to me! Say you are really alive — that you never died — !'

No word escaped her, but as she remained motionless in his desperate grip he realized that her lips had drawn back from her teeth and she was moving her mouth slowly towards his throat. She was an inch away from it when he flung her away from him in loathing. She collapsed on the stonework, rain swamping onto her barely protected figure.

'Mrs. Malden, can you not answer me?' Singh demanded, studying her with a fixed, baleful stare. 'I am Rawnee Singh, mystic. I have powers not given to most mortals. I order you to speak — to tell us the truth.'

Elsie slowly rose again from the stonework and seemed as if she were struggling to say something. She managed to jerk out a few words . . .

'Peter — beloved — In the name of God, help me now — '

She swayed visibly. Peter forgot all about the revulsion that had prompted him to hurl her away from him. To him she was again Elsie, the wife he had believed dead, chained by some unimaginable circumstance to a beyond-the-grave influence. But he did not reach her side. Before he got there something hissed out of the rain and dark and he felt a sharp stab in the arm. Pain shot the length of it and his limbs felt as if they had seized up. He dropped into darkness, his senses foundering . . .

★   ★   ★

When Peter recovered consciousness he became aware of an electric light, a

140

ceiling which needed whitewashing, and many shelves lined with bottles. Filled with a sensation of cramp he forced himself up on to one elbow. Then he gave a little sigh of relief. Seated quite nearby, regarding him steadily and yet with professional detachment, was Dr. Meadows.

'Good,' Meadows said. 'You're okay. I must have worked out the antidote correctly.'

'Antidote?' Peter rubbed a hand bewilderedly over his forehead. 'For what? How did I get into your surgery anyway? Last thing I remember I was — '

'Lying flattened out in the remains of the old chapel. I'm not quite sure what happened, but apparently there was some kind of a fight, in which Rawnee Singh was involved. Apparently it was he who fired a poisonous dart into you. Then he began to run around as though he'd gone crazy. The men on guard heard his cries and came to investigate. By the time they got there he'd gone, but you were lying unconscious. They picked you up and telephoned for me. I brought you home in my car and diagnosed the trouble. Fortunately it was a poison not entirely unfamiliar to me that was affecting you, and I made up an antidote . . . That, son, seems to be all there is.'

'But there's much more to it than that!' Peter cried, getting up slowly from the divan. 'What about Elsie? You saw her, didn't you? Or at least the guards would?'

'Elsie?' Meadows too got up. 'No, there was no sign of her. Should there have been?'

Peter groaned and beat a fist impotently against his forehead.

'Dammit, Doc, I had her in my arms. She cried out to me for help — She was alive! *Alive*, I tell you! She was cold, yes, but on such a night and in only a shroud — '

'Explain it a bit more sensibly,' Meadows insisted. 'Take it easy, Peter!'

Peter nodded wearily and began to tell his story in detail. Meadows listened without interrupting, then when it was over he fingered his jaw pensively.

'All decidedly strange,' he said at length, pondering. 'Certainly there was no sign of Elsie when the guards got to the spot. And Singh, too, had gone.'

'And you say he was running round like one crazy?'

'So the guards said. They judged it by the wild way his torch was swinging about and the cries he was giving. They knew his voice, of course. But when they arrived they found the torch lying on the ground, still lighted — but he had disappeared.'

'And they didn't try to find him?'

'You were the main concern.'

Peter was silent for a while, then he glanced up at the clock. It was half past three in the early hours.

'Thanks for saving me, Doc,' he said quietly, and Meadows merely gestured and smiled.

'I saw enough tonight to satisfy me that Elsie is alive,' Peter went on deliberately. 'I don't believe she ever really died — just as Singh forecasted.'

Meadows laughed shortly. 'That's ridiculous, Peter! I saw her die myself, and Sir Gerald Montrose verified it. You remember?'

143

'Yes, I remember, but what I saw of Elsie tonight convinces me that she's alive, but under some compelling influence. I don't think she's a vampire, either, in spite of the apparent bloodstains on her lips. Behind all this fiendish business there's a human hand. A criminal — and one of the worst criminals ever, apparently.'

Meadows motioned to the chairs again and then continued:

'Let's see if we can get some sense into this, Peter. I need to do so as much as you since, in a sense, I love Elsie — or else her memory — every bit as much as you do. You say that Singh forecasted that Elsie would *not* die?'

'Not quite that, Doc. He said there would be a termination in her consciousness which, to him, did not entirely represent death.'

'Mmmm. Let us couple that with the fact that he was responsible for attacking you tonight — and what do we get? That he is at the back of everything that is going on. In other words, he *knew* that Elsie would not really die, so it was simple enough for him to forecast a state of — suspended animation, or whatever it was.'

'But,' Peter pointed out, 'you just said that you saw Elsie die. And that specialist confirmed jour opinion.'

'Medical men are not infallible,' Meadows answered. 'The way things are going it begins to look as though Elsie settled into a condition resembling death, and both I and Sir Gerald were misled. After that . . . ' Meadows shrugged.

'Well, who can say? Singh is a mystic of renown. Possibly he controlled Elsie by mind force. Possibly lots of things . . . It seems that he knew from the very moment that he set eyes on her, on the night she went to see him at the fair, what was destined to happen to her. Of course he did! It looks as if he had it all planned out.'

'But *why* for the love of heaven?' Peter asked blankly. 'What on earth is the *meaning* of this long series of shocks, the vampires, the murders, and now this poison dart in me? What is Singh getting at?'

'I don't know,' Meadows answered, 'but it's certainly time we found out. I never did trust him from the first moment he came into the picture.'

'The Yard could probably make him talk. They'll be coming over now those two constables have been killed.'

Meadows shook his head. 'I don't think the Yard will get any further with Singh than they have with anybody else. If we want the facts we'll have to get them for ourselves.'

Peter gave a grim nod. 'All right by me. Let's be on our way. Soon as we've dealt with him I'm going back to that ruined chapel to try and find Elsie. I'm sure she's hidden there somewhere, probably by men working for Singh. There are dozens of old catacombs under that cemetery.'

'It might be better,' Meadows said, thinking, 'if we finished off Singh without asking him anything.'

Peter gave a start. '*Murder* him, do you mean?'

'I am a doctor, Peter. When I come across something loathsome that can endanger innocent lives I think nothing of destroying it instantly. We know Singh attacked you, so it is a reasonable assumption that he has been at the back of everything else. Yes — I think he ought to be wiped out.'

'And how do we explain that to Scotland Yard? And how far does it get us towards the answer of this whole damnable mystery?'

'Singh must have plenty of men working for him — '

'He had at the fair,' Peter interrupted. 'You recall those Nubians? And that other dark-skinned devil who was a sort of receptionist . . . Yes, I daresay quite a few are under his orders.'

'And they are the ones who can be made to talk,' Meadows answered. 'If we give Singh any quarter, or the opportunity to talk, he might wipe us out first. I don't think we should take that risk. I'm prepared to put a bullet through him, and admit as much to Scotland Yard when the full inquiry is complete. I don't think the law will be very hard on a man who has killed such an undesirable. Anyway, I'm willing to risk it.'

Peter hesitated, debating the wisdom of the idea. Then he realized the issue was being settled for him when he saw Meadows taking a .32 automatic from the desk drawer.

'Licensed,' Meadows said, seeing Peter's look of inquiry. 'As a country doctor I'm entitled to one. Never know what I might come up against . . . ' He hesitated, then his grim face relaxed a little. 'If you have any qualms about this business, son, stay out of it,' he advised. 'I can handle it by myself. As far as that goes I'm not even sure I shall find Singh. He said he was staying with a friend just outside the village. The only person I can think of who fills that role is Henry Chalmers. He's an eccentric and deeply interested in the occult, which seems to tie up with Rawnee Singh's mysticism. Anyhow I propose to try there first.'

'I still believe it's wrong to commit murder,' Peter said worriedly. 'I think, in spite of what we think he has done, Singh should be given a chance to speak.'

'One does not argue with a man-eater,' Meadows replied, his eyes hard. 'You're a lot younger than I am, son, and because of it inclined to be tolerant. I have no such emotions. If I find Singh I shall kill him with about as much compassion as I would a mad dog. Better make up your mind. Are you coming with me or going back home?'

'If I go anywhere it will be to the chapel to try and find Elsie. You don't suppose I can rest after having seen her walking and alive, do you? Heaven knows what is happening to her while she's unprotected.'

'If you try and find Elsie single-handed you'll be asking for it, Peter.'

'But what about those men who were on guard? They're still there, aren't they?'

'No. After they'd sent for me I told them to go home. They were pretty well worn out, and it's such a ghastly night. I didn't of course know about Elsie, otherwise I'd have thought twice. My idea was to leave things until tomorrow night.'

'Oh . . . I see. In that case I'd better come with you on your hunt for Singh, but I refuse to have any part in killing him. It's your responsibility entirely.'

'I think,' Meadows said quietly, getting

into his overcoat, 'that the best thing you can do, Peter, is go home to bed. You're none too fit after that attack. Though the antidote has cured you it doesn't mean you have unlimited strength. Do too much and you might suddenly collapse. How about going to bed for the rest of tonight then tomorrow morning — by which time I trust I shall have attended to Singh and got the Yard men over here, we can make an investigation in full strength?'

'I shan't sleep,' Peter said. 'All I can do is think of her, and whatever may be happening to her — but I also realize that I might ruin things by precipitating matters. All right, I'll go home — and in the daylight we'll take action. Can't see very well what we're doing at night, anyway, and with torches we'll give ourselves away.'

'Sound judgment,' Meadows said. 'Get into your coat and I'll drive you home: then I'll return and see what I can do about Singh.'

Peter nodded, dragged on the overcoat Meadows held for him, and realized as he did so how much his arm pained him. Then Meadows led the way to the door, switched off the light, and so both he and Peter passed to the outdoors where Meadows' car stood in the lonely road.

The rain had ceased now and a freshening wind was driving ragged clouds over the nearly-full moon. Meadows glanced up at it briefly.

'Make driving a bit easier,' he said. 'Hop in.'

Peter did so and relaxed into silent preoccupation in the bucket seat. He had no further words he could find until he was alighting outside the front door of his home.

'Try not to worry too much, Peter,' Meadows said earnestly. 'I'm sure I'm right in the way I'm handling this — '

Peter did not answer. Meadows saw him look aside and give a sudden start. The next thing Meadows realized was that the dark, inscrutable face of Rawnee Singh was looking at him through the open car window, the moonlight shining on his oblique eyes.

'I think you had better get out of your

car, Doctor,' he said, a gun glinting in his hand.

Peter stepped back, keeping his hands raised. Singh motioned deliberately.

'Quickly, Doctor! In case you are wondering how I got here, I managed to open the boot of your car and hide inside. Fortunately for me you did not drive very rapidly. I knew you must eventually come out to your car so — '

Singh stopped, the noise of Meadows' automatic briefly splitting the quietness of the night. Peter saw the flash of the gun, then Singh rocked on his feet. His own weapon fell out of his hand and he collapsed motionless at the side of the front wheel.

Meadows clambered out and examined the mystic quickly. Then he straightened up.

'Dead,' he announced briefly, his face hard in the moonlight. 'I'm sorry if you don't like the swift retribution, Peter, but it had to be done.'

Peter did not say anything. He was looking at the red stain marking Singh's oriental costume above the heart. His mackintosh was thrown open around him, looking oddly like wings. After a moment or two Peter came forward and took hold of the mystic's wrist. There was no pulse beat.

'Saved me the job of trying to find him,' Meadows commented. 'I'll take him back to my surgery and the police can see him when they turn up in the morning. You might give me a hand to get him into the car.'

Peter did so, but not with any enthusiasm. At last the slumped body of the mystic, his mackintosh drawn roughly around him, was in the bucket-seat next to Meadows as he returned to the wheel.

'Try and get some rest,' he said earnestly. 'You need it after that attack tonight. I'll be around in the morning in readiness for an investigation of the old chapel.'

With that, as Peter nodded slowly, Meadows wound up the car window, reversed, and drove away towards the gates. Peter stood thinking, and frowning, then with a sigh he pulled out his key ring and let himself into the house. All was silent. His housekeeper had presumably retired long ago.

He thought briefly of making himself a drink and a sandwich, then dismissed it from his mind. He was in no mood for eating. In fact his mind was concentrated solely upon two things — Elsie, and the murder of Rawnee Singh. He was still convinced it would have been better to question him first. Of course, he *had* had his gun ready and —

Peter shook his head confusedly to himself, went up the dark staircase, and presently gained his bedroom. For a little while he debated whether or not he should undress, get into bed and try and sleep properly — then, knowing only too well that he would never succeed, he lighted a cigarette and settled down in the armchair by the window.

Almost immediately he found his mind going back over the baffling things that had happened to him. He sat gazing into the still moonlight, seeing the entreating face of Elsie in the midst of those few imploring words she had spoken; then he saw Rawnee Singh, lips tight, revolver in hand. And across the whole crazy picture drifted a vision of Elsie's empty coffin. In the dead silence Peter could hear again the queer, terrifying thud his shovel had made when it had struck the lid of her coffin.

He stirred impatiently and crushed out his cigarette in the ashtray beside him. Again he heard a thud and for the moment thought it was his imagination; then he gave a start as he realized there really *had* been a sound, and apparently it had come from somewhere outside. Instantly all his senses were alert. He hurried to the window, flung back the half drawn drapes to their fullest extent, and peered into the night. There did not appear to be anything except the tranquillity of the countryside, an impalpable mist lying over it in the moonlight.

He was on the verge of throwing the window open wide and looking outside; then changed his mind. If there *was* something there, determined to get at him, the most sensible course was for him to wait and see what happened. It would give him the opportunity to defend himself if that were necessary. So he moved back from the window and took up a position in the deep shadow by the wardrobe. Never had he regretted more that he had no gun.

After what seemed an interminable time he caught his first glimpse of something. It was fluffy and silvery in the moonlight, just above the edge of the windowsill. Peter watched it in fascination, trying to decide if it were some kind of animal — then as it came higher and changed position he realized it was blonde hair flowing free, and that Elsie's face was outside the window, her hands clawing gently at the glass as though she were in a prison from which she could not escape.

Instantly Peter hurtled from his hiding place and opened the window. He caught at her cold, trembling body and pulled her by main strength into the room. She swayed dizzily, her eyes closed. Peter stared in horror for a moment at the red smears glistening about her lips and on her even teeth; then he whirled her up bodily and laid her on the bed.

She began to move uneasily, like one in troubled slumber. Her slender arms seemed to be trying to grasp round something; her legs moved gently up and down as though, in her dreams, she fancied she were running.

'Elsie,' Peter whispered, close beside her ear. 'Elsie, it's I — Peter. Say something to me — Elsie, beloved!'

She moaned a little and tossed her head from side to side. Peter switched on the table lamp and studied her more intently. Her shroud was dry now, he noticed, which seemed to suggest she had made her journey since the rain had ceased. But the bottom of it, and her naked feet, were splashed with still wet mud.

Peter frowned a little to himself. If she had come all the way from the cemetery across fields, and maybe part of the lane, her feet would have been cut to ribbons — yet they were not. Dirty, yes, but uninjured.

'Elsie!' he insisted, gripping her icy cold flesh where it protruded from the shoulders of her sleeveless shroud. 'For

God's sake wake up!'

His insistence seemed to have some effect for she stirred and threw up her arms, her eyes still closed. Before Peter quite grasped what had happened her hands had locked at the back of his neck and he was being dragged down towards her face.

He made no immediate resistance, quite confident that he could break free if necessary. But he found that he was coming nearer those defiled lips with every second. He strained backwards, but to his amazement found the girl's apparently limp arms had supernormal strength. Though he resisted, he was powerless to prevent his lips meeting hers. It was the one thing he wished — had Elsie been his wife; but this was a ghoulish nightmare, this sudden lascivious craving on her part for his kisses. Time and again, even though he struggled, his lips were crushed on hers and from them he could detect the deadening, crippling odour of the grave itself. She was foul, unclean — something dead yet still alive.

Savagely he made to tear free but she still clung, her hands locking into his hair so that he could hardly move his head with her dead weight hanging on to it. He seized her shoulder and tried to push her away: instead she rose with him, her eyes closed, a look of speechless suffering depicted upon her features as though, deep within her brain, some desperate struggle were taking place.

Then, suddenly, all her lassitude vanished. She tugged violently and Peter found himself flung on his back on the bed. Almost immediately her slender body was on top of him, her legs locked round his, her teeth striving to reach his throat. If ever he had needed proof of a vampire he had it now.

He flung up his hands and pressed hard against her shoulders, keeping her face away. She strained with all her power so that he saw the veins start to swell in her neck. Her eyes opened abruptly and stared at him. They were blue, as they had always been, but there was a blank, dead stare in them that made his stomach turn over.

Abruptly she got the mastery. As he sank back Peter realized it was not so much that she was superhumanly strong as that he was weak — probably from the poison in his system. It was a condition of which Dr. Meadows had warned him.

'Elsie!' he implored frantically, as her expressionless face with the bared teeth came down to him again. 'Elsie, it is Peter! For God's sake — !' he shrieked, as he felt her strong teeth bite into his neck.

What happened then he was not quite sure, but there came a sudden thunderous pounding on the bedroom door.

'Mr. Malden, is anything wrong?' called the voice of his housekeeper. 'Mr. Malden! Did you cry out just now — ?'

The effect of the hammering and voice on Elsie was extraordinary. Her teeth grip on Peter's neck relaxed and she sprawled in a dead weight upon him, hardly breathing. Peter managed to get words out.

'I — I was dreaming, Mrs. Dawlish . . . Sorry to alarm you.'

'Oh; then that's all right. I expect you will have many bad nights with so much worry on your mind.'

He heard her feet go back along the landing and a door closed distantly. Perspiring heavily, aware of a warm trickle of blood down his throat, Peter forced Elsie's weight from him and reeled off the bed. Lurching to the dressing table he peered at himself in the mirror. He had received nothing worse than a skin bite, dangerously near the jugular had Elsie carried out her apparent intention. Whipping out a handkerchief he dabbed at the wound then turned back to the bed where Elsie lay limp and hardly breathing, moisture from her efforts gleaming across her forehead.

A thought was beating through Peter's mind. Her attack had ceased the instant Mrs. Dawlish had broken into the proceedings. That seemed to suggest that she had not been acting of her own volition; that some kind of mental link had snapped at the interruption. But if Rawnee Singh were the controlling medium, and he had been shot dead — ? Peter pressed finger and thumb into his eyes in weariness; then he remembered that Singh had men who probably worked for him.

The puzzle was altogether too profound for immediate solution. The uppermost thought in his mind was at this moment Elsie was with him — alive, after a fashion. It was, to him, the only thing in the world that really mattered. To keep her safe was the thing and, regardless of the danger, try and trace the spot where it seemed the villainy was centered — in the vicinity of the old chapel.

His mind made up, Peter raced from the bedroom, and down the stairs to the telephone. Whipping it up he rang Dr. Meadows.

There was a long pause and then Meadows answered, his voice sounding as though he had only just awakened from sleep.

'Yes? Who is it? Dr. Meadows here.'

'It's Peter, Doc. Look, in the face of what's just happened I'm not waiting for a party to go and search the chapel ruins; I'm going tonight. I want your help — and your gun. Elsie has tried to attack me, and from the way she failed I think hypnotism is the explanation of her behaviour.'

'Hypnotism? Elsie?' Meadows repeated hazily. 'What's happened exactly?'

Peter gave the details, and by the time he had finished Meadows seemed to have become thoroughly awake. His voice sounded crisp and matter-of-fact again.

'I'll pick up two men from the village on my way over, and they can keep an eye on Elsie,' he said. 'Then we'll head for the cemetery. As you say, maybe we'd better act. I can't understand Elsie operating under hypnotism when Singh is lying dead in my surgery. However, we'll work that one out later. Better let your housekeeper have the facts then she'll know what's going on. I'll come right away.'

'Okay.' Peter put the telephone back on its cradle and then returned upstairs to the bedroom. To his relief Elsie was lying exactly as he had left her. He had feared during every minute he had been absent from her that she might disappear again.

For a moment he contemplated her and then went to the window and looked outside. In the moonlight he beheld the most material of things — a ladder propped up against the side of the house, which Elsie had evidently used. He recalled now the bump it had made when she must have pushed it into place.

Which raised another problem. How had she had the strength to heave the ladder into position? He knew from his own experiences with it that it was anything but a featherweight. Baffling points, certainly, yet in some odd way they cleared his brain. It made him happier to think that there could be perfectly normal happenings in the midst of the other-world atmosphere in which he seemed to have existed for so long.

He turned back to the girl at last and made her more comfortable on the bed; then he hurried to the bathroom and returned with a basin of warm water and a sponge. He sat bathing her face gently and watching redness float from the sponge into the water from where he had wiped her lips. Carefully he studied the colour and then realized what it was . . . cochineal dye. A lot of the pallor in her complexion seemed to disappear too under the action of the wet sponge.

He had come to the end of his task and was drying her face with the towel when she suddenly stirred, evidently revived by the action of the water.

'Peter . . . ' she whispered, looking at him fixedly; and he felt his heart race with joy as he noticed that the blank stare had gone. Instead she was wondering, looking inexpressibly tired, but at least human.

'Elsie! You recognize me!' Peter put aside the bowl, towel and sponge and gripped her shoulders gently.

'Why — shouldn't I?' she asked in a low voice, then her eyelids drooped sleepily. 'I'm so . . . unutterably weary,' she muttered. 'Never been so . . . weary before.'

'Listen, darling, you must answer some questions,' Peter insisted, forcing her back to semi-wakefulness. 'So much has been happening — so much that has been terrible, and only you can explain it. Everybody has believed you dead, and returned as a vampire. Twice you have tried to attack me — and failed. Now I know, from your very manner, that you certainly never really died — But the vampire business: what *is* the explanation?'

She shook her head slowly from side to side on the pillow as she lay gazing at him.

'I don't know what you mean, Peter,' she said at last. 'I can only remember — strange dreams. Strange voices. I seem — ' she stopped and frowned. 'I seem to remember being given orders, but I do not remember where — or when.'

'What is the last clear impression you have?' Peter asked deliberately. 'I *must* know, Elsie! You — and other people — have been the victims of a criminal attack. In the morning Scotland Yard will want the facts . . . Tell me, what is the last thing you remember clearly?'

'You were telling me about — Rawnee Singh. Saying something about the dark arts.'

'But that was long ago!' Peter cried. 'Before you seemed to die! All the horrible things that have happened have been *since* then! Surely you can remember?'

She shook her head again and closed her eyes. Peter compressed his lips. Then drawing back the bedclothes he settled her as comfortably as possible and drew the sheets over her. He had hardly finished doing so before a hammering on the front door below made him turn. Immediately he hurried from the room and down the staircase.

Dr. Meadows was standing outside in the moonlight, two men behind him, his car waiting in the driveway.

'How is she?' Meadows asked briskly, coming into the hall.

'No longer a vampire. I'm pretty certain now that it was only hypnotic power holding her, Doc. She's normal enough, but very exhausted — and she also seems to have amnesia. She doesn't know a thing of what's been going on.'

'If hypnosis is the basis of everything, she's not likely to,' Meadows answered. 'The hypnotic subject has no idea of what occurs whilst under the influence — Oh, I managed to get these two men to give us a hand. They'll keep guard whilst you and I take a look at the chapel ruins.'

Peter glanced at the two men and nodded a greeting. They were brawny individuals, obviously connected with the land, and though unfamiliar to Peter he assumed they belonged to the little community that existed in the village.

'Is everything all right down there, Mr. Malden?' asked the anxious voice of the housekeeper from the head of the stairs.

'Yes, Mrs. Dawlish — we're coming up this moment.' Peter turned to the staircase. 'Don't go back to your room: I want a word with you.' Peter led the way up the stairs, Meadows and the two men following behind him. Mrs. Dawlish, in her dressing gown and boudoir cap looked at the quartet in amazement as they gained the landing.

'Mr. Malden, what is happening?' she demanded. 'And at this hour of the night too!'

'If you'll come along to my — I mean my wife's room and mine, I'll explain. And don't get a shock when you see her lying there in bed.'

'But — ' Mrs. Dawlish's eyes were round with wonder and alarm. 'But, Mr. Malden, your wife is — dead! Everybody knows that — '

'It was a mistake,' Peter said. 'I'll explain if you'll only come along.'

The housekeeper had little choice, so she went ahead of the four men down the corridor and, as Peter motioned, entered the bedroom. Then she stood staring fixedly at Elsie as she lay fast asleep.

'It's impossible!' Mrs. Dawlish declared.

'You can't deny the evidence of your own eyes,' Peter replied; 'though I can well imagine how you feel — Let me explain . . . '

And he did so, in detail, whilst Dr. Meadows made a cursory examination of the girl and the two men from the village stood guard at either side of the doorway . . .

'Then — then what happens now?' the housekeeper asked finally, startled.

'Dr. Meadows and I are going to try and get to the bottom of the mystery. I think you had better stay in here and keep guard over my wife whilst we're gone.

These two men here will be outside the door in the passage. They'll give immediate help if there's any alarm . . . How does that plan strike you, Doc?'

'Quite satisfactory,' he agreed, at the close of giving the sleeping Elsie an injection. 'And the sooner we get off to the cemetery, the better. It can't be so far from dawn, and once the daylight comes our task will be hard with only the two of us.'

He packed up his bag and added. 'Your wife will be all right until we return, granting nothing unusual happens. She's sleeping normally enough.'

He came over to the door, gave Mrs. Dawlish a nod and an encouraging smile, then motioned his two men out into the passage.

'One of you keep touring the house,' he instructed. 'I don't see how any attack can be made with Singh lying dead in my surgery, but we can't take chances. Whichever of you stays here must answer any call for help Mrs. Dawlish may give. It's up to you: we'll be out of touch until we've got to the bottom of this business

. . . Now come on, Peter: the time's getting short.'

He hurried to the staircase, Peter keeping up with him. When they had reached the hall and Peter grabbed his mackintosh and hat Meadows asked a question.

'Sure you feel fit enough for whatever may be ahead of us?'

'Even if I didn't nothing would turn me back now. Let's get going.'

Meadows led the way outside to his car and Peter closed the front door behind him. In another moment or two Meadows was driving through the big gateway into the lane. His manner was taut, nervy, which, considering the strain under which he was working, with hardly any sleep, was not surprising.

'Now we can talk freely,' Peter said, his eyes on the moonlit lane ahead, 'what do you think about Elsie?'

'She's alive — and with care can be completely restored,' Meadows answered. 'Her present low condition is only the outcome of the ordeal through which she has passed. Once she begins to recover strength she'll probably be able to explain a good deal of what's happened to her. She won't remember it now, her mind still being hazy, but given time her memory will fill in the gaps.'

'I've been trying to imagine,' Peter said, 'how hypnosis could work on her with Singh lying dead. Suppose we were mistaken in him and that the culprit is somebody we've never even glimpsed so far?'

'As to that,' Meadows said, thinking. 'Singh might have given her post-hypnotic orders before he died — and at the appointed time Elsie obeyed.'

'To the extent of putting a heavy ladder against the house side,' Peter said grimly. 'I'm convinced she was *brought* to the house, Doc, by somebody — perhaps in a car. Her shroud and feet were not indicative of a woman who had struggled through fields and along a lane full of sharp stones, like this one.'

'The whole damned business still founders in mystery,' Meadows said, sighing. 'Let's hope we can find something in the chapel ruins, even if we are risking our lives by exploring . . . '

With that he became silent. The gap in the cemetery railings was only a few yards ahead. In another moment he pulled up the car and climbed out into the lane . . .

7

Within The Catacombs

'Ready?' Meadows asked, as Peter got out of the car on his own side and came round the bonnet.

'And waiting. I only wish I had a gun.'

Meadows took his automatic from his pocket and held it in readiness.

'So long as I have,' he said. 'Come along . . .'

They squeezed through the gap in the railings and, after stumbling over several graves, reached the more or less open space that led to the ruin of the old chapel. Without a word they progressed, mud oozing over their shoes, the light of the moon reflecting from a myriad small puddles where the rain of the night had not yet been absorbed.

'There's the wall,' Peter said at last, pointing. 'When I saw Elsie the first time she appeared round the far end of the old

174

cloisters, so somewhere around there seems to be the place we want.'

'Good enough,' Meadows murmured, tugging a torch from his pocket. 'We'll see what we can find.'

Once they had got beyond the wall they moved more cautiously, picking their way amidst the loose stones on the quadrangle floor. All the time they glanced about them expectantly, wary of any sudden attack — and the moonlight was a considerable advantage to help them see the surroundings. But nothing happened, so finally Meadows risked switching on his torch and casting the beam on the ground when the end of the old cloisters had been reached.

'Look!' Peter said abruptly. 'In this wet mud here.'

Meadows studied the spot and nodded. 'Definitely Elsie's footprints,' he agreed. 'Now let's see if we can discover where they go.'

Since they had come to the end of the old cloisters there was nothing ahead of them but the burial grounds studded with the white teeth of the tombstones, and here and there a massive colonnade to denote the mausoleum of some individual more important than the rest.

'Only thing we can do is see if these prints go anywhere,' Meadows said finally, and he started off again with his torch beam inspecting the wet ground before him. Peter followed behind him, double-checking on the prints. Then presently he stopped.

'More prints than Elsie's here,' he said quickly. 'There are boot marks, similar to those Singh and I discovered. No doubt belonging to the same men.'

'Not a very remarkable discovery on Singh's part,' Meadows said dryly; 'since he knew exactly what was happening. Better see where they go.'

They were not hard to follow. Elsie's prints were mixed up with them, which seemed to suggest she had been compelled to move with the men. They stopped finally at the base of a huge tombstone.

'This doesn't make sense,' Peter said, puzzled. 'How could they come to a blind end right here?'

He peered at the inscription on the stone, nearly eroded with rain and wind. It referred to a name that meant nothing. He began to examine the stone intently. It fronted to a small, long neglected grave. The prints themselves finished at the back of it and all endeavours to pick them up again seemed to be useless.

Finally Peter pushed the stone, without any hope of anything happening. To his surprise, however, he felt it move very slightly.

'Something queer!' he exclaimed excitedly, as Meadows watched him. 'Give me a hand . . . '

The doctor nodded, pocketed his torch and automatic, and came forward. With his own weight and Peter's pushing on the stone it began to tilt, and as it did so the grave in front of it sank downwards, but none of the soil in it moved.

'It's a trick grave, or something,' Peter said, pausing for a moment in amazement. 'That soil must be treated so as to cake it together solidly and the whole thing is on a fulcrum, shaped like a letter 'L'.'

'And that isn't all,' Meadows said, pulling out his torch and flashing the beam. 'Take a look there . . . '

Peter fixed his gaze on the space that the sunken — or rather tilted — grave had left. There were worn steps leading downwards into darkness.

'We've found it,' he exclaimed in sudden excitement. 'It must be a stairway leading to the old catacombs under this burial ground. The footprints vanish on the other side of the stone to make it look more puzzling in case they were found. All the owners of the feet had to do was step up onto this prepared soil, which leaves no prints anyway, and then go down the steps. I suppose the grave can be shut from below.'

'You mean going down?' Meadows asked, taking out his automatic.

'Having got this far do you think anything would stop me? Let's go!'

'I'll go first,' Meadows said. 'I've got the gun.'

He moved round to the steps and then commenced to descend them cautiously, his beam flashing on ancient, mildewed walls as he went lower. Peter kept close behind him; then when they had reached the tunnel floor they both stood looking at a big iron bar, apparently not of very great age, hanging down before them. It was curved rather like a flattened 'U' so that it could be grasped at any point when moved,

'This must close the grave,' Meadows said. 'And I think we'd better — at least until we've finished exploring.'

Peter gave a nod, grasped the bar, and pulled on it. By leverage the bar moved and at length there came a thud from the top of the steps as the specially prepared grave closed back into position.

'Nicely arranged, whoever's behind it,' Peter murmured, looking at Meadows in the reflected torch light.

'Uh-huh . . . ' Meadows flashed the beam overhead so that a monstrous, well-oiled cylindrical bar became visible, deeply sunken into cemented holes in the wall.

'The further we get,' Peter said, 'the more the business smells of organized crime. Singh certainly made a thorough job of things. He must have been around this district a great deal more than anybody imagined.'

'We'd better see where the tunnel takes us,' Meadows said, and began to move forward, torch in one hand and automatic in the other.

The tunnel extended a considerable distance before it ended at a massive old door made of teak. The hinges were solid brass.

'Looks like the entrance to some long forgotten mausoleum,' Peter murmured, studying it. 'And from the look of things nothing short of dynamite will open it.'

'Perhaps,' Meadows said, and seized hold of an enormous old ring at the side of the door. He twisted it and from somewhere there was a click. The door began to open slowly inwards, not creakily like a door that has not been budged for ages, but on well-greased hinges.

When it had swung to its limit a dim yellow glow became obvious. It was like a small oblong and apparently quite a distance away.

'A door blocking another tunnel,' Meadows said. 'And at the far end of it there seems to be life. I'd better go first and keep my gun ready.'

He went on swiftly up the vista, Peter following behind him. The yellow oblong became discernable finally as an open doorway, the yellow light deepening and brightening until it became clear it was actually from electric light globes, probably yellow-shaded.

Ten yards from the doorway Meadows stopped. Peter stopped too, trying to see what was in the space beyond, but a screen had been contrived to prevent such a possibility. There were sounds, however — metallic in the main, and there was also a throbbing of machinery, which, from its rhythm, seemed to suggest electric energy.

'How the devil could anyone use electricity down here?' Peter muttered at length, turning. 'The chapel hasn't got anything brighter than candles. I know that for a fact.'

'Only way to find out about that is to go in here and see if we can take them by surprise,' Meadows answered. 'You willing to take the risk?'

Peter nodded, so Meadows crept forward ahead of him. When they came beyond the tall screen that had hidden the view Peter stood looking about him in amazement. Though the huge space was obviously an old-time mausoleum, all such obvious signs of it being so had long since disappeared.

There were no sarcophagi, no stone tombs, but a wilderness of machinery which, basically, reminded Peter of a distillery. There were big, swollen glass globes, which looked as though they ought to house giant goldfish; there were transparent tubes in which liquid bubbled strangely. Then there were endless numbers of vats, each of them with a tube affixed to the top. Dynamos controlled endless belts, which spun the wheels of puzzling machinery. From somewhere there was the sound of hissing at regular intervals as though a suction pump were at work.

'It looks to me — ' Peter started to say, turning to Meadows; then he paused and looked at the doctor's automatic. He was pointing it steadily.

'I congratulate you, Peter, on your nerve,' he said, that strangely hard smile he occasionally revealed now returning. 'I wondered how far you would be willing to go, and to my surprise the sky proved to be the limit.'

'But, Doc, what on earth — ?' Peter did not finish the sentence. He watched Meadows close the heavy door and thrust a bolt into place.

'Keep on walking, Peter,' he instructed. 'Into the centre of the room here, if you please.'

Peter obeyed slowly, looking at the four men who were working amongst the apparatus. They were big, well-muscled, yet to judge from their foreheads pretty intelligent too. The nearer Peter came to them the more he could detect how cruel were their faces.

'Stop,' Meadows ordered at length. 'And you can lower your hands, Peter.'

Peter did so and turned to find Meadows putting his automatic away. He glanced about him.

'Do you like my factory?' he asked dryly.

'Factory?' Peter looked at him in blank wonder. 'But what in hell is all this about? I thought you — '

'You thought I was on your side. Yes, I know. No, Peter, I was never that — never from the moment you came into the picture and took Elsie away from me. I told you how much I love her. Remember?'

'Of course I remember! But you said you were so much older than she that you were glad I'd stepped in.'

'My dear Peter, don't be so naive. I hate you, and always have. I'd have wiped you out long ago only it did not quite fit in with my plans.'

'So that's it!' Peter tightened his lips. '*You*'ve been at the back of everything! But why, in heaven's name? What on earth's the idea of this set-up?'

Meadows indicated the enormous globes in which liquid frothed and foamed.

'See that?' he asked. 'It looks like port wine, doesn't it? It isn't though. It's blood.'

He stood grinning ghoulishly as Peter looked up.

'This is a converter plant,' Meadows went on, half sitting on a nearby bench whilst his assistants resumed their mysterious tasks. 'I freely admit I do it all for money, and like most things in this world anything that has money in it involves a certain amount of risk. I have taken plenty of chances to get this factory going. Smuggling machinery, acting the part of the nice village doctor . . . But it's been worth it. It is making me a fortune.'

'You mean blood is?' Peter asked hazily.

'After it has been treated, yes. Some time ago, when the vampire business first came up, I mentioned to you — in a quite unguarded moment, I must confess — that my blood-capsules were making quite a comfortable income for me. I meant it. The one thing that makes them so beneficial is the fact that their basic ingredient is genuine human blood, so treated with other chemicals that analysts have not suspected the truth. That was when I took my biggest risk — when I submitted the capsules to the public analysts for their blessing before putting them on the market. I got away with it, but so great was the demand I began to run low on supplies of basic blood.'

'Now I begin to understand,' Peter whispered. 'The vampire business was a cover-up. All you wanted was enough bodies to supply blood and you couldn't do it openly because that would have been murder — so the vampire business began.'

'Exactly.' Meadows was smiling broadly. 'Rather ingenious, don't you think?'

'Ingenious!' Peter cried, 'Why, you're nothing but a fiend! You must be to think up such a plan!'

'I have benefitted the world,' Meadows answered, preening himself in his ego. 'Thousands, unaware of what they have consumed, are in better health than they have ever been. As a doctor, that to me is the main thing. What are a few lives against the recovery of health for thousands? I have a wonder formula, Peter, and I was prepared to kill if need be to make it work out. It has been well worthwhile. I have made a fortune, and I shall go on making one. That is assured. The only two people who looked likely for spoiling me were that damned mother-in-law of yours, Mrs. Burrows — and Rawnee Singh. I took steps to dispose of them. Which leaves me free.'

'No it doesn't.' Peter shook his head deliberately. 'The Yard will find you before you're through, and you'll be hauled into court as the most diabolical murderer of all time.'

'The Yard? Those fools?' Meadows raised his eyebrows and laughed cynically. 'They're utterly bogged down, Peter, and will remain so. I have laid my plans too well for them to upset them. And you will certainly never tell anything because you won't leave here. The only other person who might have done so was Elsie — and now even she cannot because when I gave her an injection tonight I poisoned her!'

Peter was silent for a moment, absorbing the words; then as their full meaning struck him he flung himself forward and gripped the sadistic doctor by the throat. Almost immediately however he was whirled back by the assistants and held tightly.

'Naturally, that disturbs you?' Meadows

asked, loosening his collar. 'I expected it would. It disturbs me, too. I *had* planned to keep Elsie alive and marry her later, but evidently it is not to be. As I said tonight, had she been allowed to recover, she would have remembered events down here. I had planned to bring her back here, you see, after she had killed you, but things went wrong. The hypnosis under which I placed her was broken — by that housekeeper of yours. After that I could only behave as the genial doctor once again. My only way then to keep her quiet was to administer poison . . . By now,' Meadows finished, looking at his watch, 'I am afraid she will be dead.'

Peter was breathing hard. 'You filthy, no-account devil! Twisting things round from the very beginning — blaming it on Singh and shooting him . . . '

'He was dangerous, Peter. His gift for seeing into the future disturbed me. I soon realized he had divined most of my secret, so it was necessary to shoot him. I would have preferred an arranged 'vampire' attack but that could not be managed.'

For a long while there was silence, except for the rumble of the machinery. Peter stood looking at Meadows with an expression that was half horror and half incredulity. Then he shook free the hands of the assistants.

'You don't have to hold me,' he snapped. 'I know when I'm licked . . . What I don't understand is why you tell me all this? You could have shot me at any time on the way here. Why didn't you?'

'I enjoyed seeing you walk to your death,' Meadows explained, 'and also, when your blood-drained body is returned to the cemetery for others to find I wish to leave the appearance of a vampire attack, just as I had hoped I could fix things when Elsie attacked you in your bedroom. As for my telling you everything — Well, there is a certain delight in doing so, seeing how little you ever suspected me.'

'Obviously it's true what they say of criminals,' Peter said bitterly. 'That to accomplish a crime for its own sake is meaningless — but to brag about it is everything. You're the same as the rest of the killers — Crippen, Mahon, and all the brood, only you're about the filthiest of the lot.'

A glint came and went in the doctor's eyes. 'To benefit humanity is not criminal,' he said deliberately.

'That's only a paltry excuse. You're a *killer!*'

'Have it your own way,' Meadows shrugged. 'It doesn't make much difference, anyhow. I'm even prepared to be generous enough to explain anything which baffles you, then you can take all the answers with you to the grave.'

Peter hesitated, wondering if anything could be gained by a lightning attack. Since he was going to die anyway he might as well pass out fighting. Then he realized he would not stand the ghost of a chance. The assistants were watchful nearby, and he himself was still weak from his earlier ordeal when Singh had been his supposed attacker. No: perhaps the best course was to try and gain time and hope for a last minute rescue somehow.

'What about Singh?' he asked grimly.

'Was his forecast about Elsie phony, or what?'

'As I said at the time, I believe it was genuine. He foresaw that her life was in danger, as indeed it was, because I had planned what I was going to do . . . Anyway, before she came into the picture, George Timperley was my excuse for killing off people. He was removed from his coffin secretly — a death mask was made in plaster of his features, and one of my men here — approximating George in physical dimensions — became George Timperley thereafter, wearing a shroud and the death mask. He wore a rubber covering over arms, shoulders and legs, which would give a deathly flabbiness to anyone seizing him. He was also impregnated with chemicals to give that deadly, foul odour of the grave. Messy for him — but essential, eh Harry?'

The assistant addressed as Harry smiled crookedly.

'Well worth it, Doc, for the benefit we get out of it.'

'Then it was this man who attacked Madge Paignton, killed Mrs. Burrows, and then attacked you and me?' Peter demanded.

'Of course. I got myself involved purposely so as to allay any suspicion against me. The deaths of the two men after Madge Paignton were also the work of Harry here. He carried apparatus with him for draining off the blood of his victim. It was pumped back to here by a buried pipeline running through the cemetery. In cases where he was too far from the cemetery to use that method two other assistants were nearby with containers. All very thorough you see. Naturally, Timperley was kept out of his grave until such time as he had served his purpose. Then Elsie took over.'

'I assume,' Peter said, 'that it was this assistant of yours who attacked Elsie whilst I was with you that night?'

'Certainly it was. He punctured her neck and injected a slow poison, which brought on wastage. When Sir Gerald Montrose came into the picture I simply used another assistant of mine — not here at the moment — who is an

192

accomplished actor. The famous 'specialist' was, of course, a fake — but because there seemed no reason to doubt his veracity in view of my own reputation in the village, he was believed by the coroner.'

'No trick you didn't think of!' Peter cried, clenching his fists. 'Double dealing and trickery from start to finish.'

'An intelligently contrived plan,' Meadows corrected. 'Naturally, Elsie was not poisoned sufficiently to cause death. I gave her drugs that gave the impression of death, or rather a form of catalepsy, in which her heartbeats dropped to almost zero. A medical man could have detected them, of course, but no medical man was called, outside the phony Sir Gerald. Certainly *you* believed Elsie was dead.'

'Then?' Peter asked stonily.

'She was buried.'

'Which is the part I do not understand. How could she possibly come back to life after that?'

'Her condition was such that she used up hardly any air because of her low breathing rate. There was enough in the coffin to satisfy her until we got her out — '

'Singh swore that she never *was* taken out!' Peter cried. 'And I don't believe he was a liar.'

'Quite the contrary,' Meadows said. 'Let me show you something . . . '

He motioned, and Peter followed him across the great underground room to an electrical switchboard. The movement of a lever started a motor into action. Following Meadows' pointing finger Peter watched an iron elbow gently lowering a piece of the old mausoleum roof — a roughly shaped oblong, to commence with — then it took on the form of an enormous deep box. By the time the elbow had lowered to its limit there was visible a mass of soil inside the 'box,' and on the top of it some graphite chippings and faded flowers.

'God, it's Elsie's entire grave!' Peter cried.

'Just so — with the coffin still inside it, empty. When the grave site was chosen, which fact I knew a day or so in advance, of course, I discovered it was exactly over this old cavern and factory of mine. I realized it would save a lot of trouble to lower the coffin to us instead of digging it out by night as I had originally intended. So with electrical cutters we carved through the thin rock roof and, just outside the grave sides — so as not to be visible, drove in those planks you see. In other words Elsie's coffin was put into a box disguised as a grave, and then lowered down here. We got her out, returned the grave into position, and there we were. If you look above you will see the sky, as it appears from the base of the open grave.'

Peter looked and saw the dim grey streaks of dawn in the sky: then the view was cut off as the grave was returned into its position by the mechanical arm, like a lift rising into its shaft.

'In Timperley's case we had to dig each time,' Meadows said. 'Now you know why Singh did not see anybody near this grave. We did it from below.'

'And held Elsie under hypnotism?'

'I did, yes. In her semi-cataleptic state she was an easy subject to control. My main purpose was to make her kill you so that I could blame your death on to a vampire — and use your blood, of course. The first time you were with Singh, when he started investigating those footprints. On that occasion I did not return to my home, as I said I was going to do. I left my car with its lights off further up the lane and hurried by a detour to this hiding place of mine. I knew that Singh would not let anything rest and so I resolved that Elsie should seem to be the means of killing you and him. I sent my men up to keep watch. When they told me you were nearing the old chapel wall I hypnotized Elsie and she left this retreat and appeared in the cloisters, her appearance conforming to that of a vampire.

'Apparently, though, Singh had strong hypnotic powers too. He broke my hold over Elsie by speaking to her and almost making her normal. Ready for this possibility one of my men fired a dart into you, Peter, and you collapsed. It contained a powerful drug that made you weak for hours afterwards. However,

Singh was able to make good his escape and did not reappear until we were at your house — where I shot him dead.'

Peter did not say anything. Point by point he was absorbing the story and classing Meadows more as a madman with every passing second.

'I tried again.' Meadows said. 'When I had dumped Singh in my surgery I returned to here and drove Elsie to your home. I put a ladder against your bedroom window — unfortunately I may have banged it a little too hard and alerted you — and gave orders for Elsie to kill you. Under my control she *would* have done, because I knew your strength had been weakened by the way I'd drugged you. However, once again hypnosis was interrupted by your house-keeper.'

'But I rang you up at home and you answered!' Peter snapped.

'Not very difficult,' Meadows answered. 'I had a hitch-wire onto your house phone, outside. I fixed it in case a call went out to me reporting your death: that it was you who reported Elsie's return and collapse did not make any difference. I answered just the same — and I knew that things had gone wrong again. So I got back quickly to my car, picked up two from the village who work for me, and left them to 'guard' Elsie. Then we — you and I, that is — came here. Simple, isn't it?'

Peter moved slowly, hands dug deep in his pockets. He was turning the whole hideous business over in his mind. Then he asked a question.

'When Mrs. Burrows was attacked by the supposed George Timperley, how did Timperley — or rather your man — know when to attack her, and where?'

'I was at Elsie's bedside, if you remember. I had been planning for some time to get rid of your mother-in-law, and that night had been chosen. My man was ready. He only needed to see a light flash at one of the windows to know when to attack. I managed that with a fountain pen torch, which Elsie did not notice in her low condition. As for which room Mrs. Burrows was in, I assume my friend Harry here judged it must be the drawing room because of the lights being on.'

'Right,' Harry agreed. 'Killing that old battleaxe was the easiest job of the lot. Her blood was drained off by these two boys here after I'd killed her. By that time the Doc was about ready to 'find' her.'

'Why,' Peter asked dully, 'did you spare me in the cemetery when I was with Singh? Why only poison me? You could have killed me, and done with it.'

'That would have demanded firing a gun and giving myself and the boys away. Besides, the noise Singh made, and his calls for help, brought the other cemetery guardians on the scene. I made good my escape so I could be called from my home to come and attend to you. Elsie was quickly brought down here by my men.'

'Of all the ghastly, diabolical tales I ever heard, this has them all beaten,' Peter said at last. 'And you are madman enough to think you can get away with it! Don't forget the trail left by your men when the constables were slain and their blood drained away. That can be followed, just as Singh and I followed it.'

'The trail will simply be obliterated,' Meadows answered, his eyes glinting.

'Have no fear, Peter . . . I have everything mapped out. This is one secret the law will never discover. Vampires are not in the ordinary routine of Scotland Yard. Singh was the main danger, but that doesn't exist any more.'

'I suppose the deaths of those two policemen were going to be blamed on Elsie?'

'Of course. My men were careless in leaving a trail . . . However it does not signify. I hope you appreciate what has been accomplished, Peter, and how clever make up and very convincing 'blood' smears on the two vampires — George and Elsie — has caused the whole village to think that vampires do exist.'

'It can't go on,' Peter said, clenching his fists. 'Such crime as this is bound to be discovered. I admit you've planned it all quite brilliantly, and spent a good deal of money on the engineering side of the villainy, but it won't avail you anything. Right down at rock bottom, it's nothing but plain hatred of me and love of Elsie that has made you do this.'

'Partly,' Meadows agreed, 'but as I have

told you, the fortune from blood-capsules has its attractions, too. I suppose it is to be regretted that the basis of the capsules demands murder so frequently, but there it is.'

'Just the same,' Peter argued, striving to gain time, 'you've cut your own throat. Elsie is supposed to be the vampire around here. Now you've killed her how are you going to explain whatever new murders there will be? You'll have no vampire to blame them on — '

'George Timperley,' Meadows answered dryly, 'will return to the rampage . . . Elsie will be found dead in your bedroom, made up again — since you have removed all signs of it — and your dead body, its blood drained away, will be found beside her. The whole village will mourn the passing of their gallant young hero who, in turn, will be expected to become a vampire once burial has taken place. You will not become one, however: George will do quite well.'

Meadows glanced at his watch and then gave a start.

'I am talking too long,' he said

abruptly. 'It will be full daylight before long and I want you back in your home before that happens — '

'You have forgotten my housekeeper,' Peter interrupted, still trying to gain time. 'She will say plenty!'

'You don't think an old fool like that is going to upset things, do you?' Meadows asked. 'By this time I imagine my men will have taken care of her.'

He turned and signalled to his assistants. They came forward quickly and seized Peter's arms. He struggled fiercely, but without avail. Meadows stood watching as his arms were bound tightly to his sides and his ankles were lashed together.

8

Final Deliverance

'I am afraid, Peter, that this is the end of the line,' Meadows said, shrugging. 'I regret it, believe me, but — '

'You don't regret anything!' Peter cried savagely. 'You're damned glad to do it! You filthy, no-account — !'

He broke off as the doctor administered a stinging slap across the face.

'I don't have to take that from you, my boy, and I don't intend to!' he snapped. 'All right boys, haul him up.'

Peter was whirled around before he could say any more and carried to a cradle nearby made of chain. The chains were fitted about his neck, waist and ankles so that when a switch on the control panel was pulled he rose horizontally into the air and remained there, hanging exactly over one of the enormous glass bowls.

'Usually,' Meadows said, coming across to Peter and feeling the point of the needle-like instrument he held in his hand, 'I let my men do this kind of work. They know it as well as I do, but since it happens to be you this time I prefer giving my special attention to you. You have never quite realized the hurt I experienced when you took Elsie away from me, have you?'

'Why don't you get some sense into that crazy brain of yours?' Peter demanded, seeing no reason that he should not say what he thought now his doom was apparently inevitable. 'Elsie was never in love with you. Her regard for you — if any — was something like that of a child for an uncle. My only satisfaction in all this is that you killed her before she had the chance to really know what a filthy devil you are.'

'Whether Elsie loved me or not does not signify,' Meadows said, testing the needle point on the back of his hand. 'I loved *her*, and nothing else concerns me.'

The root selfishness of the man was exposed in that one remark and Peter made no attempt to answer it. Then after a while Meadows spoke again.

'Yes. I think the needle is satisfactory now. Bring over the tubes, boys . . . As for you, Peter, I think I should explain that you will not feel anything painful, beyond the initial stabs of the needle, that is. As your blood is drained away — quite rapidly by suction — you will simply lose consciousness, and never regain it.'

Peter did not say anything. He lay hanging in the chains, not trying to free himself because he knew it was quite useless. Then he gasped a little as the needle stabbed his neck, first one side and then the other. It stabbed again at an artery in his left thigh; then at one on his right. For a time he seemed to be being used as a pin-cushion — Then suction cups were placed over each puncture, tubes all leading back to a queer apparatus below which, by twisting his head slightly, he was just able to see.

'Excellent,' Meadows said, laying the needle aside. 'The actual needle punctures are small, Peter, and of no consequence. It is when the pump goes to work that you will feel the blood being drawn from you, as though a thousand leeches were at work. I have never actually experienced the sensation but I imagine it must be somewhat unpleasant . . . Carry on, boys,' he added.

One of the men moved across to the switch panel.

'Oh, by the way,' Meadows said, 'I quite forgot to tell you, Peter, how all this electricity comes to be down here. I am sure you want to know — '

'Stop playing around and get the job done,' Peter cried hoarsely. 'How much longer do you think I can stand this sort of thing?'

'I use a water-turbine,' Meadows explained, quite unmoved. 'Not far from here there is a powerful underground stream flowing through one of the catacombs. Very convenient. It supplies me with all the power I need — '

The end of his sentence was suddenly drowned out by a shattering explosion. At the same instant the door of the old mausoleum was blown clean off its hinges and came hurtling forward. It smashed into a bench, overturning it and flinging globes and bottles in all directions.

Meadows twirled in amazement, his hand clutching down to his pocket for his automatic, but he was not fast enough.

'Hold it, Meadows!' a voice snapped through the fast dispersing smoke. 'One move and I'll shoot you . . . '

Meadows, his face grim with anger and surprise, raised his hands slowly, and behind him his assistants had to do likewise.

'Rawnee Singh!' Meadows gasped at last, as the figure came forward into the full light, a group of some five men in mackintoshes and soft hats behind him.

'Surprised?' Singh asked, all traces of his peculiar studied English having vanished. 'I thought you might be! Perhaps there are one or two tricks on the board which even you haven't yet mastered, Meadows — We'd have been here sooner only we had to go back to the car for explosive when we saw the kind of door we were up against. We could hear your pretty speech plainly enough, though — and if ever there was a complete confession of crime, that was it. These Yard men are all witnesses to what you said.'

'Yard men?' Meadows repeated, still unable to realize what had happened.

'Get Mr. Malden down,' Singh ordered, and within a matter of minutes Peter found himself lowered and the tubes were withdrawn from the punctures about his body. Of the punctures themselves he took little heed since no blood had been drawn.

'How on earth did you get here, Singh?' he demanded, casting away from him the last of the ropes. 'I saw you shot dead, and you had no pulse beat . . . Anyway, I'm going,' he broke off. 'Explain things to me later: I've got to see if there is not some way in which my wife can be saved from — '

'Your wife is sleeping quietly, Mr. Malden,' Singh said. 'We saw to that — Take a seat, man! You must be all in after what you've been through.'

Singh pulled up a bentwood chair and motioned to it. Shakily Peter sat down.

'Then Elsie is *not* dead?' he asked anxiously. 'The doctor here told me — '

'He didn't succeed,' Singh said. 'I'll explain in a moment. Right now, Dr. Meadows, I'm charging you with the murder of — '

'Save it,' Meadows interrupted. 'It'll take too long to list the victims. I'm not such a fool that I can't see when I'm caught — Just tell me one thing. How do you still come to be alive? I *know* I shot you, and there were no heartbeats.'

'So, the man who creates vampires and can use hypnosis was deceived by a simple trick like that?' Singh smiled coldly. 'It is a stunt often used by fakirs, Doctor, and one which Singh himself passed on to me in case, during an emergency, I might need it. It is accomplished by a rubber ball squeezed between the arm and body which slows down the action of the heart by pressing on the great artery, thereby making a pulse beat undetectable. Illusionists and fakirs have used it for ages.'

'From — from Singh himself?' Peter repeated blankly. 'You mean you're — '

'I'm Walter Harrigan, sir, special investigator from Scotland Yard. These are

Yard men, too, all under the orders of Chief-Inspector Rushton. He's at your home at the moment.'

'Oh . . . ' Peter gave a bewildered look about him.

'I can understand you faking death, but not the bullet I put into you.' Meadows said, obviously still baffled by this one particular riddle.

Walter Harrigan shrugged and from Meadows' pocket he took the automatic he had been carrying around with him. Quite deliberately Harrigan fired it at the Doctor's chest — but nothing happened after the explosion of the gun.

'Blanks!' Meadows exclaimed in amazement. 'Then the one I fired into you was a blank?'

'Certainly it was. When I escaped from the cemetery my first call was at your home. I knew you'd probably try and kill me somehow and I didn't put a gun beyond you. I found it and, having blank replacements for most types of guns, I fixed yours. Believe me, I'm not a small-time investigator, Meadows. I've been working on your case for years.'

'But this business has only been going on for some months,' Peter pointed out. Harrigan glanced at him and shook his head.

'You're wrong there, Mr. Malden. It commenced many years ago back in Ireland, where Dr. Meadows — under a different name — had a small practice. There were a lot of mysterious killings attributed to a man reputed to be Meadows' cousin. The Irish police suspected murder. Then Meadows vanished and we found he had come to England. After that it was a case of tracing him. I was put in charge of the case and finally I located him in Little Payling here.'

Peter nodded slowly, recalling the somewhat rambling tale Meadows had once told him concerning his experiences in Ireland. Meadows himself did not say anything. He stood with his hands in his trouser pockets, the frozen smile back on his face.

'I don't quite see how Singh fits into this,' Peter remarked at length.

'Singh?' Harrigan gave a shrug. 'The police questioned him very closely and we

211

decided I might be able to get into close touch with Meadows, and remain undetected, if I took the place of Singh. Singh's permission was sought and he agreed. He told me everything he had foreseen and I practiced his mannerisms. My first move was to call at your home and see you, Mr. Malden, stating that I had got the date wrong in regard to your wife's apparent death. After that I stayed beside you Meadows, as much as possible, endeavouring to learn all I could about your movements. I didn't know where your hideout was, which was the one thing I wanted to learn. My efforts to locate it, with Mr. Malden, failed. I'm referring to earlier tonight, of course. You attacked, Meadows. I had to get out quickly or be caught and lose all chance of success. So I kept a watch on your home, Meadows, knowing it would be the place from which I could detect what happened next.

'To my surprise you brought Mr. Malden to your home. I had expected you would have dealt with him on the spot. I suppose you had your reasons. Anyway, when you set off with Mr. Malden in your car I went along with you hidden in the boot, as I told you at the time. When you stopped, I got out and took a chance on nailing you — but you shot me. Since I'd already prepared your gun that didn't signify. I simulated death, using a pellet of dye to give the impression of a bullet wound. I was ready for every trick you might pull. I knew that in the dim light you wouldn't look too closely for a bullet hole.

'After that you took me to your surgery and there left me — fortunately — quite convinced I was dead. The moment you left I followed you. Once again I was at the back of your car. You stopped at the cemetery and for the first time I saw where your hideout was. I didn't attempt anything then. Single-handed, I knew I didn't stand a chance. Instead I put through an emergency call to the Yard, asking for men right away. I'd just finished the call when I saw your car go past and I caught a glimpse of Mrs. Malden, in a shroud, in the front seat next to you. I followed on to the house.

Since I had to walk it took some time. You were leaving in your car when I got there. Before I had found my way into the house you came back again with two men. I waited to see what happened, and you left with Mr. Malden. Then I forced my way in, got the two men who had been left on guard at the point of my gun, and locked them in another room. After that I had a look at Mrs. Malden.'

Harrigan reflected, then continued, 'Your housekeeper deserves the credit for saving your wife, Mr. Malden. At one time she was a professional nurse. She diagnosed your wife's dangerous condition so I telephoned for a doctor to come over from Branwick, the next nearest town. I explained the trouble and he arrived just in time to save your wife from sinking out.

'Then I had to wait for the Yard men, but by using a 'plane from London to Branwick, and then coming to Little Payling in a fast car, it didn't take them very long. The rest you know.'

'Congratulations,' Meadows remarked dryly. 'I assume you also have hypnotic power since you revived Elsie in the cemetery far enough to bring her to the verge of normal?'

'I temporarily freed her mind, yes,' Harrigan admitted.

Peter got to his feet slowly and gripped the investigator's hand.

'Just how much you've done tonight, Mr. Harrigan, you'll never know,' he said quietly. 'And now I *must* be getting back to Elsie. I — '

'Time we *all* got out of here,' Harrigan interrupted. 'All right, Meadows, on your way. You other two men go in front.'

Meadows shrugged and began to move, but before he had got to the door he suddenly swayed, held his throat, and then pitched on to his face. Instantly Harrigan was beside him, turning him over. Then he compressed his lips.

'I should have thought of that,' he said bitterly. 'Poison. He must have slipped a tablet in his mouth while I was talking to you, Mr. Malden.'

Peter said nothing. He looked at the dead face of Meadows and then turned away. He was not thinking of the sadistic doctor or the deserved fate that had overtaken him: he was thinking of Elsie, at home waiting for him. In a few more weeks she would be completely recovered and their life could really begin with the horror forever lifted from it.

CLIMATE INCORPORATED
THE FIVE MATCHBOXES
EXCEPT FOR ONE THING
BLACK MARIA, M.A.
ONE STEP TOO FAR
THE THIRTY-FIRST OF JUNE
THE FROZEN LIMIT
ONE REMAINED SEATED
THE MURDERED SCHOOLGIRL
SECRET OF THE RING
OTHER EYES WATCHING
I SPY . . .
FOOL'S PARADISE
DON'T TOUCH ME
THE FOURTH DOOR
THE SPIKED BOY
THE SLITHERERS
MAN OF TWO WORLDS
THE ATLANTIC TUNNEL